"You have beautiful eyes." He clicked off a couple of pictures.

He hoped he'd captured the startled look on her face. It was so real, so innocent. Then her face contorted into the strangest expression.

"Do you do that to everyone?"

"What?" Jordan lowered his camera.

She pointed at the camera and waved her finger back and forth. "This. . . Just snap pictures of people without their permission."

"Sorry. I love your eyes. They're incredible."

Rose crimson filled her cheeks. He started to aim but lowered the camera. He slid off the hood of the Jeep and stood beside her.

He fought the urge to raise the camera.

She looked away. "I'd better get going."

"Randi." He reached out and caught her wrist.

She pulled away and ran down the road. He'd done it again, become too personal with a stranger. *Why, Lord? She is incredible. But I've photographed beautiful women before. I don't understand what's going on here. If I didn't know any better, I'd say I've fallen in love and want to make this woman mine. But that's foolish thinking. Forgive me, Lord. Forgive me, Randi.*

LYNN A. COLEMAN lives in North Central Florida with her pastor-husband of thirty-two years. She has three grown children and eight grandchildren. She enjoys writing for the Lord. She is the cofounder and founding president of American Christian Fiction Writers, Inc. Currently she is the E-Region director of the Florida Writers Association. Lynn enjoys hearing from her readers. Visit her Web site at www.lynncoleman.com.

Books by Lynn A. Coleman

HEARTSONG PRESENTS

HP314—Sea Escape
HP396—A Time to Embrace
HP425—Mustering Courage
HP443—Lizzy's Hope
HP451—Southern Treasures
HP471—One Man's Honor
HP506—Cords of Love
HP523—Raining Fire
HP574—Lambert's Pride
HP635—Hogtied
HP728—A Place of Her Own
HP762—Photo Op
HP772—Corduroy Road to Love

Trespassed
Hearts

Lynn A. Coleman

Heartsong Presents

I'd like to dedicate this book to all the helpful friends on the T & TTT forum. You've been so incredibly helpful to my husband, Paul, and me as we've set out to build our own Tiny Travel Trailer. Thank you.

A note from the Author:
I love to hear from my readers! You may correspond with me by writing:

> **Lynn A. Coleman**
> **Author Relations**
> **PO Box 721**
> **Uhrichsville, OH 44683**

ISBN 978-1-59789-889-8

TRESPASSED HEARTS

Scripture taken from the HOLY BIBLE, NEW INTERNATIONAL VERSION®. NIV®. Copyright © 1973, 1978, 1984 by International Bible Society. Used by permission of Zondervan. All rights reserved.

All of the characters and events in this book are fictitious. Any resemblance to actual persons, living or dead, or to actual events is purely coincidental.

Our mission is to publish and distribute inspirational products offering exceptional value and biblical encouragement to the masses.

PRINTED IN THE U.S.A.

one

"Randi!" Dorothy Grindle hollered from the back kitchen.

Randi spun around. Her foot caught, and the bowl of lobster bisque dumped all over a customer.

He jumped from his seat.

The bowl bounced on the old floorboards. "I'm so sorry." She patted the man down with the towel she wore on her apron.

"Miranda Blake, you did not do what I think you just did," Dorothy spouted as she hurried to the man draped in lobster bisque. He was well-groomed, apart from the soup. "I'm so sorry. Your meal is on us. Feel free to go home and change. We'll serve you up something special."

Randi felt the stab of Dorothy's penetrating gaze. She needed this job to hold her over. Her home Web-page-designing business was not flourishing as she had hoped it would. "I'm sorry, Dorothy. I must have tripped." Randi scanned the floor, looking—hoping—for something that would have made her lose her footing.

Clearing his throat, the customer said, "I'll clean up in the bathroom. Do you have hand dryers?"

"No, but I can lend you a clean apron to cover the damp area. And some clean towels to mop up the soup."

His brown hair, not too much shorter than her own, draped to just above his shoulders, and swayed with the nod of his head. "Great."

"Great" was not how Randi would describe his demeanor. "Controlled annoyance" fit better. The pants he wore were casual but on the upper scale of quality fabric. His wristwatch was modest, but the polo shirt and Top-Siders spelled money and summer tourist through and through. Not that Squabbin Bay received many tourists. From time to time, though, a few sailboats would pull into the harbor and spend a night or two in the area.

"Hey, Randi," Jess said with a wave as she marched in and plopped herself by a bay window. "How's it going?"

Randi shrugged her shoulders.

Jess raised her right eyebrow but didn't say another word.

Randi and Jess had been best friends since fourth grade. Jess's father had recently married one of the newest residents of Squabbin Bay. And Randi couldn't be happier for the two of them. Wayne Kearns had been the youth leader when she and Jess were growing up. As an unwed father, he had raised Jess on his own since he was eighteen. His past experience regarding sex before marriage had been a tremendous deterrent for the kids in high school. At least it had been for her and Jess.

"Randi, you can't mess up again. Once more and you're out of here. I can't afford a clumsy waitress," Dorothy muttered in a low whisper, as if to keep the customers from hearing the reprimand.

"I'll do better. I promise," Randi replied. After the lecture and cleanup, the customer still hadn't returned from the men's room. Randi took out her pad and went over to Jess.

"What would you like, Jess?"

"Nothing. I came here on an errand for Mom."

"Oh." Randi slid the ordering pad into the pocket of her apron.

"What happened?" Jess asked.

Randi slipped a stray hair behind her ears to keep it from falling in her face. "I dumped a hot bowl of lobster bisque on a customer."

"No." Jess chuckled. "Please tell me you didn't?"

"I did."

"Girlfriend, you've got to be more careful. You've got the

only available job in town. Dorothy doesn't have time to train you."

"Don't remind me. She does just about every day." Randi scanned the room and visually checked on her customers. "So what's this errand for your mom?"

Randi's joy over the closeness Jess shared with her step-mother, Dena, couldn't be more complete. In the private conversations Randi and Jess had had over the years, Jess had wondered what her real, biological mother was like since she'd had virtually nothing to do with Jess's life. Now she had a woman she could talk to. Randi was relieved because she felt inept to guide Jess in her decision to continue dating her college boyfriend, Trevor. He just seemed so strange. But Jess loved him. And Randi hoped that was all that mattered.

"I'm meeting a new photographer she's interviewing," Jess said.

Jess had gotten her dream job straight out of college, but it hadn't worked out. In less than a month, she had returned disillusioned and content to stay in Squabbin Bay. Therein was the rub with Trevor. He preferred the city life in Boston and wanted her to move back. Jess hardly spoke about him.

The customer emerged from the men's room. The wet spot on his shirt and pants was enormous.

"Excuse me." Randi ran to the kitchen and procured a clean apron and some fresh towels for the poor man. Returning with the items in hand, she stepped up to his table. "I'm sorry," she said again.

"It's over, end of story. Can I have another bowl of lobster bisque?"

"Coming right up." *And hopefully not on top of you again.* Randi grinned while placing his order back at the kitchen window. Even with the huge wet spot, he was more hand-some than any man should be, at least to her way of thinking. Randi gave a sidelong glance in his direction. She'd love to run her fingers through his wavy, brown hair. Normally men with longer hair didn't appeal to her, but there was something about his— Randi cut off her thoughts. He was good-looking. She had noticed. That was the end of it.

Jess walked over to the stranger's table. "Excuse me. Are you Jordan Lamont?"

"Yes, are you Jessica Kearns?" he asked.

"The one and only." Jess plopped herself down at the man's table.

What was his name? Oh, yeah, Jordan. Randi decided the best order of business was to mind her own and try not to lose her job. She should be able to do that for three more hours, she hoped, and fired off a prayer.

≈

Jordan felt so foolish sitting there wearing a big white apron. The lobster bisque would stain unless he had a chance to wash his clothes. His overnight bag was in the trunk. Dena Russell had offered him the spare room in her house for the night after their interview, but he would smell horrible and look even worse. The only redeeming factor was that Dena's stepdaughter, Jess, was now aware of what happened.

He needed this job. Thankfully, he'd left his portfolio out in the car. No telling what the lobster bisque would have done to it. Oddly enough, if the waitress hadn't distracted him so much, he would have moved out of the way before the bowl fell in his lap. She had a stunning beauty, her skin tone suggesting a rich Italian heritage. But what intrigued him the most was her eyes. If he wasn't mistaken, they were charcoal gray, almost black. It had been a long time since he'd seen eyes that dark.

"Hello? Earth to Jordan." Jess Kearns's voice broke in on his musings.

"Sorry. What did you ask?"

"If you'd like to have them make your order 'to go' so you can get out of those wet clothes and change at the house, that might help."

"Yes, yes, that would be great." Jordan jumped up and banged into Randi's tray.

He saw Jess's eyes widen saucerlike a millisecond before he felt the heat of the soup pour down his back. He spun around, and the look of horror on Randi's face said it all. Jordan couldn't contain himself and laughed out loud. "I'm so sorry." He helped steady Randi on her feet. "I was going to say make that order 'to go,' but you just did." He kissed her cheek and ran out the door.

As he approached the back end of his Jeep, he took off his wet shirt. Opening his tote bag, he grabbed a new polo shirt and pulled it on. Brushing his hair with his fingers, he fastened it with the elastic band he kept on his wrist.

Jess came up behind him. "Follow me," she said then jumped into a green pickup and turned on the engine.

He hesitated. He should go back and apologize again. And why did he kiss the waitress? He shook off the further need to apologize, slipped behind the wheel, and followed Jess down the winding roads that covered the Maine coastline. They passed a field of boulders. It looked as if someone had been planting them—there were so many—and yet he knew they were just part of the natural setting that made up Maine. He loved the rocky coast and wanted to paint and photograph as much of the area as possible. But that would only happen if he managed to get the job with Dena Russell, now going by the name of Dena Russell Kearns.

He could have managed to find the place on his own except for the last turn. There were no real markers to offset the turn toward Dena's home.

He'd driven by her studio in town. It had a large plate-glass window, but other than that it appeared to be a small Victorian cottage on stilts built into the rock cliff that lined the north side of Main Street.

Jess brought her truck to a stop on the broken shell drive-way and hopped out. "Bring in your bag!" she called out and marched to the side door of the house.

They had a great view of the ocean. Jordan stepped out of his Jeep and took in a deep pull of the salt air. It felt good, cool, crisp, with just enough salt and not a lot of low tide.

"Mom, I found him!" Jess hollered as she walked through the door.

Found me? As if I was lost? Grr. Not a good thing for a man who's trying to be hired as a photojournalist. Why hadn't I insisted on finding the place myself?

A woman stepped to the door. "Jordan, I'm Dena. It's good to meet. . ." Her words trailed off as she glanced at the apron around his waist.

"Sorry. I met a clumsy waitress."

"It was Randi," Jess supplied, suppressing a chuckle.

Dena smiled. "The guest room is straight back and on your right." She stepped inside and allowed Jordan entrance into the cozy cottage.

"Thank you. I'll be out in a moment."

"No problem. Would you like some iced tea?"

"Yes, thanks."

Jordan continued down the hallway to the first room on his right. He overheard Jess say, "I'm heading back to the studio to finish the bookwork."

He shut the door and placed his duffel bag on the bed of the small but comfortable room. A window faced the ocean. Jordan found himself drawn to the view. He set his hands on the sill and focused on the Atlantic past the rise of the bluff. The royal blue of the sea contrasted the sand and tall grass. He shook off the meanderings of his artistic thoughts and quickly dispensed with the damp slacks and put on his jeans. Unfortunately he had brought only one dress outfit for the interview.

He stepped out of his room and headed back to the entry-way where he'd seen Dena in the kitchen. "Hi."

"Feel better?" She placed two glasses of iced tea on the table.

"Much."

"You can wash your things later." Dena sat down at the table. "I'm assuming you passed by the studio in town?"

"Yes."

"I don't do much local business yet, but I'm working on it. Your résumé showed you had studio experience."

"Yes, that's right." Jordan and Dena continued with the formalities of the interview for the next fifteen minutes.

"So what questions do you have for me?" Dena asked.

"I'm curious as to why you're hiring someone to do the work you're more than capable of? If you don't mind me asking," he added.

"Truthfully I've cut back a lot, but I'd like to pull back further. What I'm looking for is someone who can handle the local business with an occasional photojournalism job. It takes the right kind of person to live in an area so off the beaten path. Tourism is extremely limited, compared to other areas on the coast. There are two reasons for that. One, we're much further north, so it takes a lot longer to travel here. Two, there are large tourist areas not too far from here. Personally I think Squabbin Bay is one of Maine's best-kept secrets."

Jordan nodded. The remoteness of this location had been one of the things holding him back about the job offer.

"Mr. Lamont, I've done some research on you and your work. You clearly fit my criteria, or I wouldn't have invited you up. The question is, do you think you can live in this environment? Most folks up here work two jobs. They're hardworking people with precious little to show for their efforts. That's why I'm offering the apartment on the second floor of the studio as part of the package. The lab is here in this house, which is why I had you come here for the interview."

"May I see it?" Jordan could just imagine a room the size of his bedroom having been converted into a darkroom.

"Absolutely. Follow me."

Dena Russell led him back down the hallway; but instead of turning right to the guest room, they turned left and walked past the laundry room and into one of the largest private darkrooms he'd ever seen. "Wow!"

"My husband made it for me."

He walked over to the light table. Above it were some negative strips. "May I?"

"Take a look at those." She pointed to the set farthest to his right.

"These?"

"Yes."

He turned to look for the sink and washed his hands. She smiled. Had it been a test to see if he'd reach for negatives without washing his hands? Wasn't that basic photo development 101?

Looking at negatives took an acquired skill, the ability to recognize the opposite colors for those that appeared. Oddly enough, the strip of negatives was in black and white. And the focus of the pictures looked like an abandoned fisherman's wharf.

"Print me up a couple of shots ranging from the grainy texture of the wood to the smoother, more refined photograph."

"All right. Where are your supplies?"

Dena showed him where the various chemicals were kept and the paper. She leaned against the light table and let him work. The uneasiness of the situation abated once he began the process and his mind shifted to his work. First, he made a close-up of the weathered grain of the wooden deck; then he zoomed out and re-centered the frame to slightly off to the right side of the negative and printed a full-size photo. A short time later, he put the photographs in the water bath to stop the chemical reactions then hung them up to dry.

Flicking on the normal light, he asked, "What do you think?"

"You tell me."

He scrutinized each photo but settled on the one he felt confident was the best. "This one."

"Why?" Dena stood beside him looking at each photo.

"I like the contrast. It looks kinda Ansel Adams to me."

"Interesting."

He wanted to ask. *Did I get it right?* But held off. His mind flickered back to the clumsy waitress and her wonderfully alluring eyes. He wondered what they would look like in a black and white print.

"Let's clean up and go to the studio." Dena caught him in his musings. They talked as they put everything in its place in the darkroom. She was organized, unlike him. He'd love to look through her filing cabinets and see how she organized them. That was one of his weakest areas. He had logs and notes on his laptop, but apart from setting negatives aside with the date on the outside of the envelope he didn't do much organizing. It would be an honor to work with Dena Russell, even if it was only doing studio work. Then again, he could probably learn that in a few weeks. *Would I be bored with no challenge, no adventure?*

The hard fact was he needed a steady job. Income was not what he'd hoped when he left college to pursue his career. Freelancing hadn't been as profitable as he'd anticipated. To date, he owned a Jeep, a few cameras, some tubes of paint, and an easel. And his nest egg was the size of a twig. His apartment was a room with kitchen privileges that he rented from the other two guys who leased the place. At twenty-seven, he'd hoped to be further along in a career. Far enough along where he could entertain the thought of marriage. But he barely kept himself alive. He didn't earn enough to support a wife. Not that he'd found a wife yet.

"I'm glad you handle film so well. Are you equally skilled in digital photography?" Dena asked.

"Very. When I started college, digital photography wasn't financially practical for all the students. I'm grateful I was trained in both. I use digital most of the time, but I still enjoy working with the film and always have my film camera with me."

Dena gave a slight nod. "Jordan, what's your dream with regard to your career?"

two

Randi tossed her purse on the table. *What a day!* She made it through without getting fired but only because Dorothy had seen the customer back into her serving tray and not the other way around. The man had to be a photographer, Randi figured, if his appointment was with Dena Kearns. She toed off her sneakers and pulled off her socks. Ever since she started living on her own, she found the freedom to go barefoot around the house. When she was younger, her father insisted she wear shoes all the time, or at the very least slippers, in the house. So she'd been forced to keep her toes covered for years.

She padded her way to the office, a small second bedroom. Her dad had come by and rewired that section of the cottage with up-to-date wiring and surge protection. Her computers and equipment were the tools of her trade, and unfortunately an uncontrolled charge of electricity could wipe out her system in less than a second.

Her other major expense was satellite service, giving her fast access to the Internet. Uploading and downloading took forever on dial-up. Speed and ease of working back and forth with a customer were top priority. She had lost too many customers prior to the expense. The other faster services were not available in her area and probably wouldn't be for some time. So she settled on satellite in order to continue living in Squabbin Bay. Of course, back then it had been because she believed she was going to get married. But after four years. . . well, she broke it off when she saw Cal fooling around with Brenda Scott. They married a month later, and then he split less than a year after that.

Now she wasn't sure why she wanted to stay in the area. It wasn't the fast track to success, but it was home and the place she felt the Lord would have her live. Most of her friends while growing up had moved out to go to college and simply never returned.

The phone rang. "Hello."

"Randi, you'll never believe this," her friend Susie blurted out. "There's a handsome new photographer moving to town. He's going to work for Dena Kearns and live in the apartment above the studio. I hear he's a hunk."

Susie was a bit of a gossip but always tried not to pass on bad news about others. The idea of a new man in town would have all the women buzzing.

"He is," Randi confirmed.

"You've met him? Tell me—what's he like? How'd you meet him? Are you interested? Is there room for the rest of us?"

Randi chuckled. "Whoa, girl. The man wears his hair to just above his shoulders. It's brown and wavy. I imagine he can tie it back into a small ponytail."

"Eww, I don't like men in ponytails. On the other hand, if he looks great, who cares how he wears his hair?" Susie laughed.

Randi thought back on his thick brown hair, skin tone, and the structure of his face, and her heart fluttered. "Hey, I'm sorry, but I've got a deadline, Susie. Call Jess. She's seen him."

"Sure, no problem. Talk with you later."

Randi dropped the phone in the cradle. She had a deadline, and if she didn't get this finished before midnight, she'd lose a client.

She had the new Web page design uploaded and fully functional before twelve a.m. The online appointment with her client went well. He was pleased, and the payment for the job was done immediately, also online.

The next morning, Randi set off on her daily jog around the harbor and past the inlet two miles south of her cottage.

In total it was a five-mile run. Once in a while Jess would join her, riding a bike, but the hour and the exercise didn't suit her friend. Fortunately for her, she didn't have a body that would gain weight, unlike Randi. She fought the bulge every day. She ate right, exercised, and still had to work at maintaining her weight. Sometimes life wasn't fair.

Lord, it seems some folks don't have to struggle for anything, yet I have to. Why? She ran on to the last corner before the inlet. As she turned the corner, she saw a Jeep along the side of the road and a pair of jean-clad legs stretched out on the ground beside it.

Lord, no. All those television shows of criminal science investigations flowed through her mind. She squeezed her eyes shut and headed toward the vehicle. Shaking, she pushed forward. *Lord, don't let it be a dead body. Please don't let it be a dead body.*

&a.

Jordan lay perfectly still, even though the morning dew was soaking through his clothes. He'd been waiting ten minutes for just the right shot. The nest of baby ducks, the mother hovering over her little ones, and the sun's rays bursting through the clouds would form a beautiful picture. His finger poised on the shutter-release button.

Just a moment more—that's it, Momma—move a little to the right—perf—

Crash! Thud!

Someone trampled the ground around him. "What—?" There she was again, that klutzy waitress with those wonderful dark eyes.

Jordan clicked off an accidental picture. He aimed the camera back to the mother duck and ducklings, but the shot was gone. The mother now sat on top of the nest, keeping the babies under her wings. Jordan clicked off a couple of pictures then turned toward his intruder.

"I take it you're fine," she said, huffing.

"Damp, but fine."

"Do you often lie down by the side of the road to take pictures? Isn't that dangerous?"

Jordan sat up and placed the lens cap on his single-lens-reflex film camera. It hung beside his digital camera around his neck. "Sometimes. Do you often trample over everything?"

"Hey, I thought you were—never mind." Randi stepped back. "Enjoy your day."

She started to run down the road.

"Hey, Randi, I'm sorry." Although he wasn't quite certain what he had to be sorry for. Hadn't she interrupted his shot? Didn't he have a right to be annoyed by the intrusion?

She waved but kept running. He leaned on his Jeep for a moment and watched her strides. He lifted his digital and aimed. After snapping a couple of pictures, he rounded the Jeep to the trunk where he kept his photography equipment. He thought back on Dena's office and the shelves of lenses and cameras, all neatly arranged. *If she could see my trunk, she probably wouldn't hire me.*

The interview had gone well. He and Dena Russell shared similar tastes and eyes toward photography. He realized she'd asked him to pick his favorite of the prints to get a sense of his eye.

Her vast experience of film, lighting, and settings proved he could learn a lot from her. Just her array of cameras and lenses spoke volumes. She probably had close to a hundred lenses alone. Jordan looked down at his pitiful supply in comparison. He had ten lenses, plus four cameras—two film, two digital. If he didn't count his cell phone and the Polaroid he used when painting.

Jordan sat on the hood of his Jeep and watched the golden sun rise over the horizon. Wisps of fog rose from the water.

He lifted his digital and tried to capture the soft vapors.

The footsteps of a jogger, probably Randi, approached from the direction she had run in earlier. He had to give her credit.

He found exercise boring and unfulfilling. He'd heard the talk about endorphins released in the brain from hard exercise, that it helped clear the head, helped process information faster.

"You run often?"

She crossed the road and lightly jogged in place. "Five days a week, weather permitting. Do you?"

"Only away from something," he quipped.

She narrowed her gaze.

He lifted his camera. "A bear, a moose, an occasional mountain lion, or panther."

"Really?"

"Occasionally." He held back from the urge to boast. He didn't need to impress this woman. And yet he wanted to.

"Dena's been all over the world. Have you?"

Jordan half chuckled, half snickered. "No, I've not been that fortunate. But if I understand Mrs. Kearns's history, she didn't do much until the last decade."

"True. So are you moving here?"

She stopped jogging in place and stretched. Jordan swallowed his wayward thoughts and focused his camera and his own attentions back on the stray wisps of fog rising from the water.

He decided to avoid the question, not knowing the answer himself yet. "So what do you do around here besides spill lobster bisque on people?"

He'd been attracted to this woman since he first spotted her in the restaurant. The very thought of falling for someone made his hands shake as he clicked off a shot. He groaned.

"What's the matter?"

"I messed up the picture."

"How?"

Jordan had no desire to tell her why. "Just went out of focus."

"Oh. I never could hold a camera straight. I took photography when I was a kid for 4-H, and my pictures were all blurred and washed out. I failed at developing them, too. Of course, I probably just took a lousy picture."

"What kind of camera?"

"I don't know—one of those rectangle ones from Kodak, I think. It was so long ago. When did you start taking pictures?" she asked.

"High school. Someone donated some photography equipment to our art department. The school set up a darkroom in what used to be a storage room for the science lab. Anyway, a couple of friends and I signed up. I've been hooked ever since."

"Did you go to college?"

"Yeah, but I majored in fine art. Do you know how few jobs are out there requiring that degree?"

She shook her head. She'd stopped stretching and jumping, making it easier to look back at her. "You have beautiful eyes." He clicked off a couple of pictures.

He hoped he'd captured the startled look on her face. It was so real, so innocent. Then her face contorted into the strangest expression.

"Do you do that to everyone?"

"What?" Jordan lowered his camera.

She pointed at the camera and waved her finger back and forth. "This. . . Just snap pictures of people without their permission."

"Sorry. I love your eyes. They're incredible."

Rose crimson filled her cheeks. He started to aim but lowered the camera. He slid off the hood of the Jeep and stood beside her.

He fought the urge to raise the camera.

She looked away. "I'd better get going."

"Randi." He reached out and caught her wrist.

She pulled away and ran down the road. He'd done it again, become too personal with a stranger. *Why, Lord? She is incredible. But I've photographed beautiful women before. I don't understand what's going on here. If I didn't know any better, I'd say I've fallen in love and want to make this woman mine. But that's foolish thinking. Forgive me, Lord. Forgive me, Randi.*

❧

Randi was still shaking after she got home. She'd never had a man enter her heart so quickly, so deeply, before. Yesterday the kiss, today. . . "Lord, what just happened? I wanted to jump into his arms because he said he loved my eyes. Thankfully, with Your grace, I fought it and ran away."

She still couldn't decide if she wanted him to move into town or not. At the moment she was leaning toward no, that he should go back to wherever he came from and stay out of her path.

After years of prayer for her future husband, could she sense a connection to this man that went beyond the physical? She shook her head. Should one be that connected to another so quickly? Four years of dating Cal never produced this kind of unexplained closeness. "Okay, Lord, I need Your grace here."

She got ready for work at the Dockside Grill, which years ago had been called the Dockside Café. Then Dorothy started thinking grills were more popular than cafés and changed the name. Randi didn't see much difference in the clientele.

The wall clock read eight thirty; she had two hours to work on a Web page before going to Dockside. She sat down in front of her computer and researched a potential new client's Web page. She'd been asked to evaluate it and make suggestions for enhancing and updating the Web presence of the company.

She stopped at a popular search engine on the Internet and typed in Jordan Lamont's name. She saw only one reference to a photograph—an elderly woman with well-worn skin, a Native American. Her eyes reflected the years of life, the joys, the struggles, the pain, and the glory. "How'd he do that?" she wondered aloud. It was as if she could see into the old woman's soul. There, in the refracted light of her pupils, she saw the reflection of the photographer.

Randi clicked the computer window shut and jumped away from the computer.

Her heart felt exposed. She got down on her knees and prayed for the rest of the morning before going to work. "Please, God, don't let him move to Squabbin Bay."

three

One month, two days, and seventeen hours since he'd moved to Squabbin Bay—and still no sign of Randi. He couldn't imagine a person could go unseen for such a long period of time in such a small town. He didn't dare ask Jess. Word had gotten back to him that she thought he might have been overly interested in Randi. On the other hand, he couldn't blame Randi for her concerns.

He'd asked for the Lord to intervene and keep their attraction to one another in control. He'd even gone so far as to pray for Randi daily. And with each passing day, he'd had an increasing wonder as to whether or not she was the wife the Lord had designed for him. But not to see her at all. . .

"Maybe it's for the best, huh, boy?" He rubbed the top of his dog's head. Duke's long, velvety ears flapped back and forth from the rubbing. Together he and the basset hound lay on an old blanket, eating fried chicken and watching the sun go down. He'd had to leave Duke at the apartment with his roommates during the interview. He tossed his faithful companion a chunk of his boneless portion. He knew the fried batter wasn't good for the poor creature, but Duke had a thing for chicken. So rather than have him try to eat the bones, Jordan had long ago given in to buying Duke his own boneless breast of chicken.

"She's a hoot, Duke."

Duke lapped his jowls and waited for another tender morsel.

Jordan wiped his hands on a wet cloth and positioned the camera on the mini tripod. Tonight was the first evening he'd had to relax and enjoy his passion for photography.

He was hoping to catch a sunset using a telephoto lens with a graduated neutral density filter. He focused on the horizon but not on the sun. He'd heard too many stories of photographers ruining their eyes trying to photograph the sun. The best way he could describe it was to imagine himself holding a magnifying glass between his eye and the sun. Not a comforting thought.

He set the wide-angle lens on the digital to underexpose for a more dramatic sunset—he hoped. They sat on a western bluff of the peninsula that made up Squabbin Bay. Fortunately the peninsula was long enough that only a small spit of land protruded into the horizon. Technically it was a less boring picture to have the jagged coastline jutting out into the horizon. It gave the eye something to look at besides the sunset.

A jogger ran on the beach below. The posture of her body, the movement of her legs. . . Jordan aimed the camera at the runner. A gentle smile eased up his face. It was she, finally, after all this time. "Randi!" he hollered and waved.

She came to a sudden halt and lifted her hand to her forehead, scanning the bluff above her.

"It's me, Jordan. Jordan Lamont." He paused and added, "Dena Kearns's new photographer."

She gave a hesitant wave then continued running down the beach.

Well, that's my answer. Whatever mutual attraction or connection he'd imagined they had for one another obviously wasn't the case. He'd fallen for a woman who had no real interest in him whatsoever. "Sorry, Lord. I guess I misread You. I thought—oh, never mind what I thought. It doesn't matter. I was wrong, and I will continue to wait on You for my spouse."

Jordan quickly pushed his thoughts aside and refocused on the horizon. The sun would be coming down on the right-hand third of the viewfinder just behind the shore's jutting coastline. One of the first lessons he'd learned in photography was the principle of the thirds, which really transposed to dividing the picture into nine equal parts.

The golden rays turned a variety of colors ranging from orange to purple as earth's star settled down for the night. Jordan clicked off several shots then put the equipment away. Tomorrow was his day off, and he planned to paint. It would be his first day to paint since arriving at Squabbin Bay.

He loaded up the Jeep and whistled. "Come on, boy, let's go home." Duke ambled over. Jordan had learned long ago that basset hounds preferred to think it was their idea when to do this or that. He'd also learned food was a powerful motivator. "Want another piece of chicken?"

Duke's little legs picked up speed. His ears flapped as he ran. Once he came up to the Jeep, Jordan lifted and placed him in the passenger seat then climbed in himself. He drove out the dirt road that led to the secluded spot. At the end of the road, leaning against the gate, was Randi. He pressed the brakes.

Her arms were crossed, and the look on her face seemed stern, angry almost. "Are you following me?" She pushed off the post and rounded the Jeep. "Why were you here? Did you follow me?"

He thought back on their last encounter when he had reached out and grabbed her wrist. Time told him he'd read that situation all wrong. Very wrong, according to the attitude he was seeing right now. "Randi, I don't know what you think I've done, but I am not following you."

"Oh, really? Since when do you come to this remote location? How'd you even know about it?"

"Look—I'm sorry if I've offended you. But I came out here tonight because Dena recommended it. I had no idea you would be jogging on the beach." He wanted to beg for forgiveness, but he honestly didn't have a clue as to what he should ask forgiveness for.

"Oh." She stepped away from the vehicle.

"Good night, Ms. Blake." He wanted to toss in that he'd see her around, but it appeared that would not be received as a pleasant prospect.

She nodded and started jogging in the opposite direction. Jordan drove back toward town and his apartment. His heart felt as if it been ripped out of his chest and squeezed in a vice. "Help me, Lord. I really thought she was the one You designed for me. Of course, it was probably too soon to think such a thought. Forgive me. I just got carried away."

ช

Randi felt more out of sorts than a flounder flopping on the deck of a ship. Could she have misread Jordan on their two previous encounters? Two types of people are out there, she reasoned, those who are demonstrative and those who are not. It was entirely possible Mr. Lamont was just a touchy-feely kinda guy. But. . .weren't most guys that way? Randi groaned and plopped on the overstuffed chair in her living room. To say she'd been avoiding him since he moved into town would be putting it mildly. Not only had she changed the area where she normally ran, but she also had stopped working at Dockside Grill and taken another waitress job in Ellsworth on Route 1A. And though she'd been telling folks the tips were better, and they were, she knew the real reason—and it had nothing to do with increased pay.

Jordan Lamont scared her. "Why, Lord? Why should I be afraid of this man?" *Admit it. You're afraid of your feelings for him.*

Randi let out a frustrated groan. For six weeks, she'd been dealing with this conflict of emotions, and there was still no change. She didn't dare tell Jess. After the first time of trying to describe it to her, Jess was afraid Jordan had done something inappropriate. How could she explain it when she didn't understand herself? Her head began to throb. She'd been having headaches from all her circular thinking. "Lord, take this away. It has to stop."

After freshening up from her run, she opened her Bible and scanned the pages until she fell on the verse in Philippians 4:19. "And my God will meet all your needs according to his glorious riches in Christ Jesus." *Lord, one of my needs right now is to relax around Jordan Lamont. He scares me. Not just from the attraction, but. . .oh, I don't know. . .more like he invaded my heart and mind. How can someone I just met connect with me so deeply?* After several more minutes in prayer, Randi felt compelled to apologize to Jordan and to try to get over this fear. The invigorating night air encouraged her to walk the three blocks from her house to his. Not that Jordan knew they lived so close. Her feet seemed to get heavier with each stride, but she pushed on until she knocked on the back door to Dena's studio and the entrance to Jordan's apartment.

Within moments, he stood there with his hazel eyes and long, wavy hair. "Hello, Ms. Blake. What can I do for you?"

Such formality. "Hi. I came to apologize. I shouldn't have accused you."

"Apology accepted."

"Thank you."

"You're welcome. Is there anything else I can do for you?"

Hold me in your arms. She shook off her wayward thoughts. "No, I just felt you needed. . .and I needed. . ."

"Like I said, apology accepted. I hope you didn't lose your job at the Dockside Grill because of me."

Randi let out a nervous chuckle. "No, I found another job. Actually I only waitress to bring in a little extra income. I'm a Web-page designer."

"Really? How much do you charge?"

Randi outlined her fees and services.

"I might just hire you. I've been meaning to put together a site on the Internet for myself. What does something like that involve?"

"It all depends on what you want the site to do for you."

"Well, then, once I have some extra capital, we can talk and you can give me an estimate."

"Sure. I designed Dena's. You might want to take a look at it. It might give you some ideas."

He turned his wrist and looked at his watch. "Sounds like a good idea. Well, thank you for coming by to apologize, but I have to get back to my work."

"Sure. See you around." She waved and headed home. *Well, that was an awkward but congenial conversation. Why am I so nervous around him?* she wondered. What could he be working on that involved a timer? Wasn't the darkroom at Dena's house? She looked back at the house and watched the consistent flash of a strobe light. What could he be taking pictures of with that?

She stood there and watched for a moment. What was it about this man that brought out her curious nature?

A horn honked. Randi turned and gave a weak wave. *Just what I needed now—NOT!*

⁂

Jordan stepped back from his canvas. It felt good to paint again. Especially after working with the strobe lights for the dairy farmer's ad campaign. It had taken several hours to shoot the milk splashing upward in just the right pattern for an exceptional picture. He seldom got around to painting, but living in Squabbin Bay brought out his creative juices. Today he'd decided to paint an old crab shack. In years past, the shack had been the wharf where crab fishermen would bring in their catches. Today it held a small gift store and empty docks. The salt-gray weathered boards and the reflection of the building in the shallow water seemed like the perfect scene for his first painting.

His hand froze a half inch above the canvas as Randi Blake stepped out of a small, red, compact car. He watched as she stomped inside the crab shack. One thing was certain—this woman showed her emotions. A minute later, she nearly ran out of the building. Jordan dropped his palette on the case containing his supplies. "Stay, Duke."

Running around the small inlet, he reached her car just before she turned onto the street. "Are you all right?"

She jumped and turned toward him—those wonderful charcoal-gray eyes filled with tears.

"Randi?" His heart ached to show her some compassion. "Are you okay?"

She nodded and drove off.

Okay, Lamont, that was swift. First the woman is terrified of you. Last night, she apologized, and you think—what? That she'd be interested in talking with you? Telling you her woes? Yeah, right. Jordan turned back to the one true friend he had in the world, Duke. *A man can't go wrong with a dog like Duke,* he mused.

"Hey, boy, I'm back!" he called out as he rounded the bushes that lined the road between the crab shack and the driveway to a town pier.

He repositioned himself again behind the canvas and lifted his palette and brush. The sun's light had changed. Jordan considered the new contrast of shadows and decided to continue painting it with the shadows he had already begun working with. He glanced at the Polaroid shot he'd taken when he felt the lighting had been perfect. He eased out a pent-up breath. *Why did I bother, Lord?*

Ten minutes later, a car pulled up behind him and parked. Jordan didn't turn around and look. He wanted instead to capture a couple of colors before the sun and clouds shifted once again.

"You paint?" Randi's voice tickled the back of his neck.

"Yes," he said without turning around. *Relax. Stay calm.* "Are you okay?"

"I will be. I'm sorry. I couldn't talk a few minutes ago."

"Not a problem—you don't have to explain." Jordan stepped away from the painting. It was time to turn around and be friendly. The sight of her standing there nearly took his breath away. *Lord, give me strength.*

"Jordan, I'm sorry. Can we start over?"

He gave a slight smile. "Sure." He put his brush in his left hand across the palette and extended his right hand. "Hi, I'm Jordan Lamont, and I work for Dena Russell Kearns."

Randi chuckled and took his hand. "Hi, I'm Miranda Blake."

"Miranda. I like that."

"Thanks. Only my parents tend to call me that. I've gone by Randi since I was five."

"I'll call you whichever you prefer." He gently removed his hand. "This is Duke." The dog wrinkled his eyebrows and examined this new stranger. "Say hello, Duke."

Duke let out a short, bassy *whoof.*

Randi giggled. "Hi, Duke." She extended her hand, keeping her fingers curled, and let the dog sniff her before petting him. "You're a handsome fella."

"Duke loves compliments, don't you, boy?" The low-lying critter cocked his head slightly to the right.

"He's got a personality."

"Absolutely. In fact, Duke here is the king of the castle. Just ask him."

She bent down and gave him a good rubbing. "Do you take him everywhere you go? I noticed him in your Jeep last night."

"Just about. Obviously I can't take him on some trips. But any I can, I do. In fact, do you know of a good kennel around here? I have a photo op in Connecticut next week, and I need someone to care for him. I can take him to Mystic, Connecticut, and put him in a kennel there, but I'm not sure Duke wants to spend ten hours in the car to go to a kennel."

"Not here but possibly in Ellsworth."

"Okay, I'll check around." The sun had shifted too far behind him. Jordan could not continue with his painting. He reached over and placed his brush in turpentine to clean it.

Then, with a palette knife, he started to clean off the excess paints from the palette.

"I'm sorry. Did I stop you?"

"Not really. The sun has shifted. I can finish this at home just as easily as here."

"Oh. How do you like working with Dena?"

"Fine. It's a bit slow at the moment, but when we work together, I'm learning something new each time. I should have taken a job with someone like her years ago. I'd be further along in my work."

"Are you working tomorrow?"

"No, not really. Why?"

"Well, there's a carnival at the church. The youth are sponsoring—"

He'd forgotten about that. "Right—isn't that the event where Dena met her husband?"

Randi chuckled. "Yup, pie in the face, the whole bit."

"Pie in the face?"

Randi went on to explain how Wayne Kearns had crashed through the church swinging doors at the same moment Dena was going through them in the opposite direction, carrying a pie and her camera.

"Which one, 'old faithful'?"

" 'Old faithful'?" she asked.

"That's the name she calls her first SLR camera. It was a Nikon F2 photomatic. It's the camera she used to get started. It's a great old camera. Kinda wish I had one myself. But a man needs to set his priorities."

"True. Anyway, are you interested in coming? I'm working—collecting the tickets for the dunking tank."

Jordan chuckled. "I believe I heard the pastor threaten those who adjusted the switch last year so he was dunked continuously." *She attends the same church. I'll have to keep an eye out for her next time.*

"Yup. Rumor has it that John Dixon did it, but no one's

saying for sure. His wife supplied the pastor with tons of vegetables last year from their garden."

"Nothing wrong with some good, old-fashioned fun."

"So you'll come?"

Is that hope I hear in her voice? "I might make it over after dinner."

"Don't. There's sure to be enough food, and the kids can really use the income. They're planning a trip to Africa this year."

"Africa, hmm. Maybe I should volunteer."

Randi laughed. "They had more than enough volunteers until folks heard the list of rules for the guardians as well as the kids. Seriously I think they have enough. And I think you'd have to wait a year before folks would let their kids go with you. You know—you're still a stranger."

"I hadn't thought of that." Jordan continued to pick up his equipment.

Randi stepped closer to his easel. "You're good."

"Thanks. I'm fair, but I hope, given some time, I'll get better."

"I'm surprised Dena didn't ask you to help with the portraits she does. She did such an excellent job last year, and with her son being the pastor, it's a given that, as long as she's in Squabbin Bay, she'll have a spot at the carnival for portraits."

"She volunteers her time on that. I'd hate to charge her." Randi stepped back and examined him as if evaluating him. *What did I say wrong that time?*

"You haven't lived in a small town much, have you?"

"No. Does it show?"

Randi chuckled. "Yes. Folks around here would never have thought of charging for their part of the carnival. You, on the other hand, immediately thought of your salary."

"Hey—"

Randi held up her hand. "My point is, your thoughts went to salary, payment for services rendered, stuff like that. Here we don't really consider it, unless we're doing our jobs for hire."

He felt reprimanded, but he wasn't certain why. All he said was he couldn't charge Dena for his services at the carnival when she wasn't getting paid herself. *What's wrong with that?*

"I'd better get going." She turned to walk back to the car.

"See ya around." He smiled. There was something about this woman. He was beginning to feel like a boat's motor oil spilled out in the water, totally unmixable and plenty chaotic. How could he ever have thought they were meant to be together? Jordan blinked as he caught a glimpse of those amazing eyes watering once again.

four

Randi sat behind the table at the ticket booth and scanned the festival again looking for Jordan. Her heart sank a fraction of an inch. Still no sign of him. She'd hoped he'd come and join in. If the man was going to blend in, he needed to become an active part in community events. *In my not-so-humble opinion,* she thought.

"Miranda!" Her mother waved.

Randi smiled and waved back. Her mother led a group of small children over to the hippo pen. Cardboard-painted creatures drank at the fake river. Papier-mâché heads popped through the surface of the water. And on the opposite wall, one could sit on a hippo and have his picture taken. At another spot, a person could sit in the hippo's mouth. The youth had done a bang-up job on this African display. A collection jar for donations was a hollow palm tree with four-inch PVC pipe in the core of the tree and a slit in the trunk for people to put in loose change, bills, or checks.

Hidden in the shadows, poised with his camera, sat Jordan. Randi's smile brightened.

"Ten tickets, please." A small boy with short, cropped, blond hair looked up at Randi.

"Sure. Two dollars."

He handed her the crumpled dollar bills as she counted out the tickets. "Here you go."

"Thanks." He ran off and lined up, waiting for his turn at the tank. She noticed that the man sitting on the seat above the tank waiting to be dunked was Charlie Cross. Randi nodded. She looked back at the boy with his hand full of tickets and back at Charlie. *The boy must be his grandson.*

Her booth was a four-foot table with a wooden sign suspended overhead by a couple of thick fishing lines attached to the tree limb above her.

"Hey, Randi, how's it going?" Jess asked.

"Fine. Where's Trevor?"

"He didn't come. To be honest, it's over between us. I tried to keep it together, but he made it clear that, unless I moved back to Boston, he didn't see much sense in pursuing a relationship."

"Sorry."

Jess waved off the comment. "I'm over it. Mom and I had some long, heart-to-heart talks, and the truth is, for the past year, I've not loved Trevor the way a woman and man should love one another for a life of marriage. I tried to buy his affection when I first started working in Boston. Dad nearly flipped over that."

Randi chuckled. "I remember. What were you thinking?"

"I wasn't. That's what Mom and Dad pointed out. I did all the giving when it came to Trevor and me. He barely did anything. He hardly does anything. Do you know he still hasn't gotten a job and is living with his parents?"

"Ouch."

"Yeah. I love my parents, but I'm moving out as soon as I can put a down payment on a house. We decided that renting wouldn't be a wise investment when houses aren't selling at too high of a price right now."

"Are you earning that kind of money?"

"Almost. I'm working with the lobstermen to establish a co-op, and so far it looks very promising. By this time next year, we should be doing a good business. I hope anyway."

"Wow! I'm impressed. So tell me why I'm just hearing about this now?"

"Sorry. I've been working around the clock. We did decide to have you design the Web page, though."

"That'll be fun. Are all the locals in the co-op?"

"Just about. Dad's working on the last of the old salts."

"Have I seen you going out a time or two on your dad's boat lately?"

Jess chuckled. "Yeah. I think his taking me out there all those years got stuck in my veins. I actually enjoy pulling the pots and fetching the lobsters. Still not crazy about the chum for the bait bags."

"Eww. Who is?"

"Most get used to it."

"Eww. . .not."

"That's because you didn't get lugged out on the boat with your dad every morning until you were thirteen."

"Thank the Lord for small blessings."

After a chuckle Jess asked, "Can you come over Sunday after church for a barbeque?"

"Love to. What time?"

"One." Jess leaned closer. "Mom's invited Jordan. Is that a problem?"

Randi could feel the heat blazing her cheeks. "No."

"Good. Look—I gotta run. And you've got a line here. See ya later."

Randi nodded and went back to work selling tickets to the small line of children. By lunchtime, Jess returned to give Randi her first break. Jess sat down behind the ticket table while Randi picked out a lobster roll and a cold soda and sat at a picnic table.

"Hey!" Jordan called out. "May I join you?"

"Sure."

Jordan set his plate on the table and swung his leg around the picnic-bench seat. "The youth group does this every year?"

"Yup."

"Wow! That's amazing. Who's their art director? That hippo pit is great."

"Mr. Landers and Jan Dufresne. Mr. Landers is the high

school art teacher, and each year one of the events is a project for the entire art department."

"Awesome. I saw fiberglass and papier-mâché."

"The fiberglassing is done by the shop teacher. That's where Jan comes in."

"You have a lady shop teacher?"

Randi chuckled. "Yeah, Jan's father was the shop teacher for many years. But he retired three years back, and she took over the job. She'd been working as his assistant for five years before that. Now her oldest son is helping. I can imagine one day he'll be the shop teacher."

Jordan took a huge bite of his lobster roll and nodded his head slowly as he chewed. His wavy hair flowed gently back and forth across the top of his shoulders. A sudden urge to run her fingers through his hair emerged again.

"What?"

"Nothing." Randi ate her own sandwich to keep herself from laughing.

"Come on. It was something. Am I wearing my food? Do I have a huge chunk of mayonnaise on my face?"

She placed her sandwich back on her dish. "No, nothing like that. That was a huge bite of sandwich."

"Oh, well, I was hungry, and I love lobster." He picked up his sandwich and bit off another huge mouthful.

"I can tell."

"Do you?"

"Yes, but I've had it all my life. To me, it's like hamburger. Dad's a lobsterman, so we ate it several times a week. That and a lot of flounder. Those would get trapped in the pots, and Dad would bring them home for dinner. It was a real treat to have hamburgers or spaghetti." She took another bite, about a third of the size of Jordan's.

"Wow, I can't imagine."

"You know, back in the early part of the 1900s folks didn't eat much lobster. The market was horrible. I've heard the pioneers thought lobsters were for poor people."

"I'm not big on history. I only know what I've seen, and in New York City, I saw lobster selling for thirty bucks a pound. It was nothing to see a restaurant charge over a hundred bucks for a lobster dinner."

"Now that amazes me. As much as I consider it hamburger, I don't think I would pay a hundred bucks for one lobster."

Jordan's laughter calmed her. The more she talked with this man, the more she wanted to get to know him. Not to mention, the more she felt as if she already knew him. She sipped her cold drink.

"Nor would I. I haven't had much lobster until I moved up here."

"Watch the cholesterol if you add the butter."

"You eat lobster without butter?"

"Yup. You're eating it now without butter."

"I know, but that's because it's chopped up and cold. But. . . is it good?"

She gave the top of his hand a patronizing tap. "Yes. I'm sorry; I have to go. Jess is just watching my booth until I'm finished with my lunch."

"No problem. I want to mingle some more."

She stood up and paused. "Are you enjoying it?"

"Yes. And I'm getting to meet some of the people, especially the parents of little children. They're potential customers for portraits."

Randi sighed. "Bye." He just didn't get it about money and community. She wondered if he would ever truly fit in.

❧

He'd done it again. What, he wasn't quite sure, but he'd seen that look on Randi's face before. Jordan went back to his lobster roll and continued to observe the people. He certainly understood why folks enjoyed this fund-raiser for the teens. He'd really like to volunteer to be a chaperone, but Randi was right. People didn't know him yet and might have reservations about him being responsible for their children.

Jess came over with her own lobster roll. Since he'd come to work for Dena, Jordan found Jess to be a new friend. She'd come in to work on the studio bookkeeping while he was there. Not to mention the meals he'd shared with Dena, Wayne, and Jess at their house. "How's it going?"

"Fine. What are you responsible for today?"

"I worked before the festival to bring in enough lobsters and other seafood. Tonight we're planning a campfire down on the beach for the youth. Dad, Mom, and I went there at dawn to dig and lay out the stones for the clambake. Have you ever been to a clambake?"

"No, I can't say that I have." Jordan sipped his drink.

"They're awesome. First you dig a hole and layer the hole with rocks, generally round or oval-shaped, about the size of a football. Then you build a fire. It has to burn long and hot enough that water drizzled on the rocks will sizzle. You then remove all the coals and coat the rocks with six inches of layered seaweed. The clams go down first, then the lobsters, and on top of that you place the corn, potatoes, sausages, and so on. You cover it with canvas, and in about an hour it's all done. The key is getting those stones well-packed and very hot."

"Seems like a real art form."

Jess shrugged. "Goes back to the Pilgrims—and they learned it from the Indians."

"I've heard of a clambake but just never participated in one."

"Unfortunately tonight's bake is for the teens. It's Mom and Dad's way of thanking and encouraging the youth."

"Your dad used to be one of the youth leaders, right?" Jordan picked up the camera and took a couple of candid shots.

"Yeah. I don't know if he did it to keep me out of trouble or just because he had a passion for the teens. I think it was probably a touch of both. Once I went to college, he turned over his part to Bob Hackett, who became the church's youth pastor."

Jordan wasn't sure whether he'd met Bob yet or not.

Jess took a hearty bite of her sandwich. He did the same and finished his.

"Thanks for sitting with me. I guess I should do some more mingling. I took a few pictures of the kids playing in the hippo pool. I hope we might get some potential customers from that."

"Whoa, dude. Jordan, you have to stop thinking of this community as potential customers. Granted, they will be, but you can't think of them in those terms. I know Mom wants to see the studio succeed, but she's not interested in a huge profit thing. Think in terms of getting to know folks. Let them get to know you. That will bring in business around here, not regarding them as potential consumers."

Jordan nodded his head slowly. "Ah." *Is that what Randi reacted to earlier?* "Thanks for the tip."

"No problem. Relax. Don't stress about making such a great impression on my stepmom. She's cool, and she's happy with your work."

Jordan smiled. "Thanks."

"No problem. Later. I have a meeting with the town selectmen."

He knew Jess had a degree in business, and he knew she'd been organizing a co-op with the lobstermen of the area. She was a smart gal for someone so young. And she hit the nail on the head concerning his issues of finances and putting them in the proper perspective. God had been dealing with him about that for years. His wants, his dreams, and his general lack of funds. . .well, maybe not lack of funds—but certainly no extra.

He scanned the area and focused on Randi sitting behind the table. The wind gently blew the sign back and forth above her head. He raised his camera and zoomed in. Suddenly he noticed the line holding the sign. He dropped the camera that hung around his neck and ran as fast as he could. He tackled Randi to the ground just as the sign crashed on the table.

"Are you okay?" He brushed the hair from her face. Her deep, dark eyes opened and closed and then slowly opened again. Tiny flickers of gray in her eyes became clearer. His heart thundered in his chest.

Her eyes widened. He realized he was holding her down and jumped up. "I'm sorry," he mumbled.

Others were running over. "What happened?"

Jordan offered Randi his hand. She placed her shaking hand in his. "Thank you," she whispered.

He didn't know if it was for the hand up, for removing himself from her, or for saving her from a horrible injury. "Thank the Lord I made it in time." He turned to the gathering crowd. "The fishing line that was holding the sign broke."

"How'd you see that?" an elderly, heavily jowled man asked.

"I caught it in my camera lens. It magnifies well."

A woman Jordan knew he'd seen before spoke up. "I reckon Randi's mighty pleased by your rescue. Not that you had to tackle her as if you were at a football game. You okay, Randi?"

"I'm fine. I might bruise, and I think he knocked the wind out of me."

The crowd chuckled. Then Pastor Russell spoke up. "Better the wind than you being seriously injured." He turned to Jordan. "Thanks for being quick on your feet."

Jordan cleared his throat. "The Lord had His hand in it."

"I do believe you're right." The pastor slapped him on the back then turned toward the gathering crowd. "I need a volunteer to get a new table out here and another to take down the other line."

A few of the men jumped up and helped. Two guys put the broken table in someone's pickup truck. Whether it was going to be repaired or taken to the dump, Jordan didn't know and, quite frankly, wasn't concerned. What kept going through his mind was how scared he'd been for Randi. Not that he wouldn't have reacted the same way for someone else, but the instantaneous thought of possibly losing her ran deep. So deep that it unnerved him.

After the crowd dispersed, she came up to him and placed her hand on his arm. "Thank you."

"You're welcome."

"Jordan," she whispered, "I think we need to talk."

He agreed, but he couldn't talk yet. How could he explain to a near stranger how instantly and deeply he'd fallen in love? He couldn't. "Possibly later. I need to get back to the studio. It's been closed longer than I planned."

"Okay, later." Randi walked over to the new table.

A middle-aged couple came running up to her. "Miranda?" She embraced the woman, whom Jordan assumed to be her mother.

If time and place were different, he'd love to be alone with her, to open his heart to her. But that terrified him, as well. He walked to the studio from the church. "Lord, help me here."

five

"I'm all right, just shaken." Randi straightened her blouse and prepared to sit down behind the new table.

"What happened?" her father asked.

"Jordan Lamont, Dena Kearns's new employee, saw the string slipping or something in his camera and tackled me to the ground."

"Were you hurt?"

"No, Mom, I'm fine."

"Where is he?" her father asked.

Randi turned around, but Jordan was no longer there. "He's gone. He said he had to go to the studio and open it up."

"Ah, I'll speak with him later. You're all right?"

"I'm fine, Dad."

"Okay, then, I have to go back to the sack races. I'm calling the next event."

"I'll see you later."

Mom sat down beside her at the table. "I know you're all right physically, but you seem pretty shaken up."

"I am."

"You should be. Come have an iced tea with me." Her mother found someone else to take her place with the children, and they moved over to the refreshment area, purchased a couple of iced teas, and sat down at a private table. "Honey, you've been a little edgy ever since this Mr. Lamont moved into town. Has he done or said anything we should be concerned about?"

"No, Mom. He's fine. It was me. . .I guess. I don't know. He's very demonstrative."

"How so?"

43

"Well, the first time I met him, he kissed me on the cheek. That's after I spilled the lobster bisque on him a second time."

Her mother giggled. "I'd forgotten about that." Her mother paused then continued. "It is alarming that a man would kiss a stranger, but if he's, as you say, demonstrative, maybe it is just his way."

"I figured that, but I don't know. There's something more. He sets me on edge."

"Hmm." Her mother examined her a bit closer.

Randi looked down at her lap. "I'm attracted to him to the point of its being unnerving. The second time I saw him, he reached out and touched my arm. The intimacy was so deep it scared me."

"Ah."

"Mom, it's as if he trespassed into my private thoughts, into my heart. It was scary."

"Yeah, I imagine it was. You know, we haven't spoken much about your broken engagement and what happened between you and Cal. I think it might be time."

Randi scanned the area to see just how private their conversation could be. "There's really not much to say. Cal was a cad, and Brenda got what she deserved."

"Possibly. But there is another side to that coin. What about the fact that God may not have wanted Cal to be your husband? You assumed that because you two were so compatible, it was natural for you to get married. Your father and I were thankful you both wanted to wait until Cal finished college. We felt it would give you time to realize Cal wasn't the right man—or us time to discover the potential in him as your husband. In the end, Cal wasn't the right man."

"Mom, I know all this. What does it have to do with Jordan?"

"Patience, honey. I'm getting to that. You and Cal were not as close as you thought. You were friends, but not as close as, say, you and Jess. A husband, to my way of thinking, needs to be your best friend. Cal wasn't that. Is it possible you and Jordan could be developing a friendship?"

"We are," she blurted out. "I mean, I realized I was wrong for being afraid of him, and I've tried to speak with him on more than one occasion."

"Good. I'm not saying Mr. Lamont is going to be your husband. I'm just curious about why you felt so vulnerable to him."

Randi's eyes widened. "I don't know."

"Well, pray about it. I've got to run. Thank Mr. Lamont for me for saving your life."

"Sure."

"Be careful, Miranda. Trust your better judgment."

The rest of the afternoon, she thought back on her mother's challenge regarding her past relationship with Cal. She thought about how Jordan had come to her rescue and how secure she felt in his arms. Something she hadn't felt since Cal had betrayed her.

Yes, she and Jordan had a lot to talk about. If only they could find the time and the right setting in which to do it. She was concerned about being alone with him. Not that she didn't trust him, but because her heart felt so vulnerable.

And what was his problem that he had to work 24/7?

ॐ

Inside his mailbox Jordan found his first forwarded bill from Boston, his cell-phone bill. He slipped his jackknife in the extra-thick envelope and sliced through the paper fold. His eyes widened upon seeing the total amount due. "Three hundred and twenty dollars?"

He scanned the myriad of pages and discovered the problem. He was in an area that wasn't covered by his network's roaming fees. Unfortunately he wasn't prepared for that kind of expense this month. Moving had taken a greater portion of his savings than anticipated. Not to mention the new equipment he purchased before coming because he felt it would help him do his job better. He looked at the new 500mm zoom lens he'd just received in the mail. "Lord, should I return it or simply fast for most of the month? Not that I'm trying to make light of fasting, and I definitely could spend more time in the Word and in prayer, but. . ."

His glance flickered back to the bill. He pulled out his cell phone and called the three-digit number that connected him with his service provider. Fifteen minutes later, he had managed to get through all the sales pitches and canceled his phone service. And since he hadn't renewed his agreement last month, he wouldn't owe a fee for stopping it.

He'd have to shop around for the best service in this area.

Shaking off the unpleasantness of remote living, he pulled the digital cards from his cameras and went to work developing the candid shots he'd taken at the festival. No sooner had he loaded the images than the bell jangled over the front door to the shop.

"Hello?" a female voice called.

Jordan turned. "May I help you?"

The red-haired lady sported a healthy shade of sunburn pink on her nose and cheeks. She wore a white skirt; a striped, navy top; and Top-Siders. "I was wondering if you process digital pictures within an hour?"

"Sure can. Load the images you want printed over there." Jordan pointed to the equipment that stood against the right wall. "Or you can hand me the card, and I can take care of it for you."

"No, thanks. I'll do it myself."

"No problem. Give me a holler if you need anything."

" 'Kay."

He judged the woman to be in her early thirties.

Jordan went back to his pictures. He cropped the photos for the best four-by-six prints. He'd learned long ago to photograph a larger border on digital cameras because the enlargement process was limited to multiples of four-by-six, and an eight-by-ten could not provide a perfect ratio enlargement.

The sweet, toothless grin of a child filled the screen. She seemed familiar, but he couldn't place where he'd seen her before. Of course, with a town as small as Squabbin Bay he'd probably seen her around on more than one occasion. He printed out a four-by-six and moved on to the next print.

"Excuse me."

"How can I help you, miss?"

"How soon will these prints be ready?"

"Less than an hour. You can return later if you like."

She stepped back then paused. "Does anyone else work here?"

"No. Well, yes. My boss. But she's busy with the festival. I'm the only one today. I wasn't even open until a few minutes before you arrived."

She glanced out the front window. "All—all right," she stammered. "I'll be back in an hour."

"I'll have them ready for you."

Jordan worked on his own prints, processed a few new orders from customers then gathered the photos together for the lady's order. He thumbed through the prints, checking for quality. Seeing no problems, he set them in the envelope for small pictures and rang up the printed label, with the price tag sealing the envelope shut.

"Hey, Jordan." Randi swung open the door. "What are you doing here? Why are you working?"

"I wanted to get a start on some of the pictures I took today. It's a good thing. I've had a half dozen customers this afternoon."

Randi placed her hands on her hips. "Has anyone ever told you that you work too much?"

"No, but I take it you're about to educate me."

"How'd you guess? Come on—you're coming back to the festival with me."

"Sorry, but I can't. I have a customer who's returning for

her prints. She should be here any minute."

"Fine." Randi leaned against the counter and crossed her arms. "I'll wait. Then you're closing shop and taking the rest of the day off. After all, you saved my life today, and you deserve to have some fun. You know the Lord talks about taking a rest every now and again."

"I rest."

Duke howled then, as if to protest.

"You tell 'm, Duke. Look—I've seen you for nearly a month, working every spare minute. And when you're not working, you're painting. One or the other. In either case, it is still work."

"Painting is my hobby."

"Not! You sell them. It's another form of income for you. What do you do just for fun?"

Jordan thought for a bit and realized he couldn't remember the last time he'd actually taken time off.

"See—I've got you. Now it's too late to dunk you in the tank—"

He waved her off. "Hang on. What do folks our age do around here?"

"Travel to see the movies, do something in the city. Whatever. We also get together at each other's homes. Truth is, there aren't too many of us. Most of the kids I went to school with left town for college, and they don't return, except for visits."

"Go to which city, Ellsworth?"

"Yes, have you been?"

"Can't say that I have."

"Do you like bowling?"

"Haven't done that since I was fifteen, but I'm willing to give it a try. What about shooting some pool?"

"Tim Redcliff has a billiard table in his barn. He makes it available for folks."

"You up for a game? What about asking Jess to join us? Or is she going to the clambake after the festival with her parents?"

"Don't know about Jess. Let me call Tim; then I'll call Jess."

Jordan nodded and finished his prints. He sorted through his pictures, and the sweet smile of the toothless gal landed on top of the pile. While Randi continued with her phone call, he enlarged the copy and printed out an eight-by-ten.

The red-haired lady from earlier ran in the door. "Sorry I'm late."

"No problem. That will be six dollars and forty cents."

"Here—keep the change." She plopped seven dollars on the counter, swooped up the envelope, and hustled out the door faster than she'd come in.

Randi clicked her cell phone shut. "Who was that?"

"I have no idea. Hey, who do you have cell-phone service with? I just got my bill, and I need to change providers."

They chatted while he cleaned up the area from his work.

"Jess can't make it."

Jordan paused. *Is it wise to be alone with Miranda?*

six

Randi watched Jordan as he worked. He was so methodical, taking the time to put everything in its right place then tweaking it until it stood in perfect line or the order he wanted. She wagged her head involuntarily. This model of orderliness didn't jibe with the clutter in the back of his vehicle. "Are you always this precise?"

"Huh?"

"The back of your Jeep looks like everything was just rifled through and piled on top of each other. The counters of this shop are in pristine order. Who's the real you?"

"Ah, this is for Dena. Have you ever seen how organized that lady is? I mean, everything is in its place. I'm haphazard at best."

"Dena is organized in her lab. But her paperwork. . .well, let's just say it took two weeks before the papers, prints, and everything were well-organized in her new lab."

"Really?" Jordan's shoulders relaxed.

"Jess said when she lived in Dena's apartment in Boston the house was organized and clean, but her bedroom, which also served as her office, was overrun with papers everywhere."

"Done." Jordan beamed. "Are you sure you're up for a game of pool? Are you sore?"

"A little, but I'll be fine."

"We don't have to play tonight. You're under no obligations because I saved your life."

Randi giggled. "Not according to the town. Besides, we have some unfinished business."

"Ah, the talk."

"Yes. What happened between us today when you"—Randi

scratched quote marks in the air—" 'rescued' me from that sign?"

"Are you sure you want to get into this conversation? You always seem to run away from me."

"Jordan, I was engaged for three years. Well, officially only one, but the other two were informal."

"Ah. I don't think this is a pool night. Let's go to the city and have a nice steak dinner, my treat."

"Really?" Her dark eyes rounded.

He reached out and took her hand. For the first time since she'd met Jordan, she didn't pull back. "Really. Call Tim and say thanks, but we've changed our plans. I'll run upstairs and get Duke some water and doggy treats."

"You're taking Duke? I don't think you can bring him in the—"

"I don't intend to take him into the restaurant. However, I've not given Duke any of my time. If he rides in the Jeep, he thinks he's spending quality time with me."

"You're a little obsessed with your dog, aren't you?"

"Probably, but he's been my best friend for years. He's a great listener, and I've never heard a rude word out of him."

She smiled then said, "I'll call Tim."

Randi paced back and forth. *What have I gotten myself into?* It had seemed like a good idea to speak with him at the festival, but now she didn't feel so sure. She flipped open her phone and called Tim. Jordan ran down the stairs and hurried toward the back door, signaling to her to give him one minute. Inside the kitchen, he pulled out a couple of bottled waters for Duke and a handful of puppy treats he put in a plastic bag.

A minute later, she'd finished her call. She closed her phone and turned to see Jordan watching her, leaning on the doorframe, looking like a million bucks in casual jeans, a cotton shirt tucked in, a belt buckle that looked as if it came from a rodeo. And his hair. . . "What?"

He gave her a lazy smile. "You're a beautiful woman."

Fire danced on her cheeks.

"Are you going to run away?"

"No, but I want to."

He moved slowly toward her. "Miranda, I—" He stopped short then stepped back. She'd never been so thankful someone moved away from her.

He cleared his throat. "I'm sorry. Let's get going to dinner. Do we need reservations? It is Saturday night."

Her tongue felt dry. "No, we should be fine. We might have to wait a few minutes. No big deal."

He nodded and grabbed the keys to his Jeep from a peg on the wall. "Let's go. Come on, Duke."

The basset hound wobbled to a stand on his short legs.

"How old is he?" *On second thought, I'm glad he's bringing his dog. It will give us something to talk about.*

"Duke is thirteen. That's ninety-one to you and me."

"Wow! He's an old man."

"Yup." Jordan scooped up the dog and put him in the backseat. "He's lived with me all his life, except for my first year in college. My folks insisted I live in a dorm the first year. After that, I lived off campus in my own apartment, if you can call rooming with four to six guys your own apartment."

He held the door open for her. Randi grabbed the roll bar and pulled herself up into the high vehicle. It wasn't as high as some of those new pickup trucks, but for someone her size, it was high enough.

"I moved out of the house last year. After Cal and I broke up, I needed to be on my own. Mom and Dad were great, but I don't know—I just wanted to be on my own."

"I understand." Jordan closed the door and walked around to the driver's side. He didn't run, nor was he being exceptionally slow, but each step he took struck her as purposeful. It was confusing, trying to piece together the many facets of this man.

Sliding behind the wheel, he turned toward her. "Which way?"

Randi fought to relax her nervous stomach. "North." With only one main route into town she didn't have to explain more, which was a blessing.

❧

Jordan pushed his chair back from the table. "That was good. How was yours?"

"Excellent."

"Would you like some dessert?"

"No, I'm stuffed. Besides, I purchased a lemon meringue pie from the festival today."

"Now that sounds yummy."

Randi's eyes widened. They were onyx in the dim lighting of the restaurant. "You like lemon meringue?"

"Yup, and just about any way pie comes. I have a huge sweet tooth."

"You don't look it."

He wiggled his eyebrows. "That's because I work 24/7, as you say."

"Why is that?"

He shrugged. How could he admit he was anxious to earn the kind of living that would provide for a wife and children he didn't yet have. *For her,* he hoped. She'd been the best date he'd ever had, and this wasn't even a real date. "I have plans for the future, and it's hard to earn a lot doing photography. Truthfully, if it hadn't been for all those roommates, I would have had to get a job to help support myself."

"Dena does well."

"Yup, but she established herself when she was married."

"Actually that isn't quite true. Jess told me that when she became a widow she used the life insurance to buy the studio with the upstairs apartment. From what I've heard our pastor say in his sermons, his mother, Dena, went through some hard times the first three years after his father died. His father was a minister also, so they didn't own their own home and didn't really have much of anything."

"I knew her husband died a while back, but I didn't realize she started her business after he died."

"Yup. Photography was just a hobby before that."

"Well, she has the eye. She's good, and her name and reputation stand for quality."

The waiter, in dark pants and a white shirt, came up to the table. "Excuse me. Will that be all for the night, or can I tempt you with some desserts or an after-dinner beverage? We have several specialty coffees."

He glanced over at her and smiled. "Miranda?"

"No, thanks, I'm fine."

"Just the check, please, and would you wrap this bone in a doggy bag for me?"

"Yes, sir." The waiter stepped away.

Jordan took in a deep pull of air and let it out slowly. "Are you still wanting to talk?"

"Honestly, no. But we need to."

"Okay." Jordan slid down to the edge of the chair, stretched out his legs, and crossed his ankles. Relaxed, he wasn't; but he wanted her to be.

"Jordan, I don't know how to explain this without being horribly blunt. I like you. But I'm terrified by you, if that makes sense."

Jordan paused for a moment to collect his thoughts. "Tell me about your engagement to Cal."

"Why? What does that have to do with you and me?"

"Perhaps nothing, and maybe everything. I don't know what happened, but I suspect he dumped you. A fool, if you ask me."

Randi wrung the cloth napkin in her hands. "Yes, he was having an affair with someone I knew. Not that it's hard not to know someone in Squabbin Bay."

"Then he definitely was a fool. How have you dealt with the trust issue? I can see you've dealt with the hurt. You've moved on and made a life for yourself. But what about trust?

Can you trust a man, any man?"

"I haven't had a problem around any other man, except you."

"Ah." *Because of that connection we felt for one another the second time we met. I know the feeling.* "Miranda, I like you. I'd like to get to know you better. Maybe over time you'll feel more comfortable around me. I'd like to be your friend."

Her eyes widened then closed. They told so much about her and what she was thinking. And he'd done it again. This time, he'd hurt her. "Friend isn't a bad thing."

She lifted her head and gave a slight smile. "No, friend isn't a bad thing."

"Okay, I'm clueless here. I would like a relationship, but I admit I'm terrified by the emotions I feel for you, felt for you from our second encounter. The first was unique—but not something to build a relationship upon."

Randi giggled. "I'm so sorry."

He held up his hands. "I know it was an accident. Let's not get off the subject. I thought friendship was a good place to start. Is there something wrong with that assumption?"

"My mom said something similar today. She thinks Cal and I weren't meant for one another, and I didn't see that."

"Is she right? I mean, it's obvious the guy was a jerk, but—"

"I don't know. I always blamed Brenda for the affair. They married a month or so after we broke up. He was engaged to me for years. And—"

"What was it in Cal that made you want to marry him?"

She pursed her lips then twitched them. "I don't know. I mean, I used to think it was what we were supposed to do. I'd loved him since tenth grade."

Jordan paused then asked, "Friends—meaning you and me? Can we be?"

"Yes. I think that's a good idea for now."

"Good. I could use a friend in town. Jess told me today I had to stop looking at people as potential customers."

"She told you that? Of course Jess would tell you that. But, yeah, you need to stop thinking that way."

"Noted. So can I consider you my second friend in Squabbin Bay?"

"Absolutely." She paused. "Second? Who's the first?"

He smiled. "Jess. Well, I think Duke is going to start howling soon if I don't return. The bone ought to help."

"Buying his affection, huh?"

"You could say that."

Randi seemed to relax for the first time all evening.

Jordan plopped a hefty tip on the table and escorted Randi from the room with a gentle touch on her elbow. He'd be the perfect gentleman. She needed a man who loved her enough to respect her. And with God's help he would be just that man. All in all, he decided, tonight had been a wonderful evening. He opened the front door of the restaurant.

"Duke? What are you doing here?"

seven

Randi moaned as she crawled out of bed the next morning. It had taken hours, until well after midnight, to recover Jordan's vehicle from the impound yard. He had parked in front of a No Parking sign. She'd never seen a sign there either, or she would have warned him.

Her head throbbed from lack of sleep. She went into the bathroom and took two aspirin. Five minutes later, she was burrowed back under the covers and asleep. The next time she opened her eyes, it was well after noon. She'd missed church. She went to her laptop and downloaded the Sunday morning sermon then uploaded it into her iPod.

Showered, dressed, and feeling a lot better, she drove to the Kearns home. Jess greeted her at the door with a tall glass of iced tea. "We'd given up hope on seeing you. Jordan told us what happened."

"I never saw that sign until we found out they towed the Jeep."

"Jordan's laughing about it. Come—there're a few morsels left."

Dena and Wayne were lounging out on their deck chairs. Jordan sat beside them with a plate full of food. She really did wonder how he stayed so thin with an appetite like his. She waved.

He returned the gesture and kept on speaking with Dena and Wayne. Pastor Russell stood at the grill. Large meat patties were lined up and at various stages of completion. "Would you like one or two, Randi?"

"Two, thanks."

"Coming right up."

"Sorry about missing the service. I listened to the first part of the sermon on the way over. Sounds good."

"Digger is doing an excellent job. I can't believe he has the sermons up and ready on the Internet before I even get home. It's amazing."

"Gotta love it." Randi smiled. She'd taught Digger, aka Tommy Williams, a teen at the church, how to upload on the church's Web page and how to write the basic computer code so folks could find it.

"Absolutely." Pastor Russell scooped two burgers off the grill and placed them on a red plastic plate.

For a moment, she watched the children running back and forth to the end of the cliff that overlooked the beach then turned to find an empty chair.

"Come with me. I've got to show you something." Jess pulled her by the arm through the house and to the kitchen. On the table lay a Realtor's printout of a house.

"Is this what I think it is?"

"Yeah. I haven't seen it yet, but at the festival yesterday the Realtor handed me this printout. What do you think?"

"I think it's way too soon for you to be considering a house, but what do I know?"

Jess giggled. "Plenty. I have time to look, but staying with Dad and Mom—"

"They're newlyweds," Randi finished the sentence for her. Her mother's words came back from yesterday about her and Cal not having been that close. She never finished Cal's sentences for him. Well, except to correct him. Randi sighed.

"What?" Jess sat down in the chair. "Come on—what's going on in there? Is it the house? Am I missing something?"

"No, no, not the house. If you and your parents think it's a good idea, go for it. No, it's something my mother said to me yesterday about Cal and me." Randi glanced down at the paper again. "Isn't that Brenda and Cal's house?"

"Yeah, sorry."

Randi waved her off. "No problem. Why isn't Brenda keeping the house?"

"She's moving closer to her mother. Apparently Cal hasn't been great with the child support."

A lump flipped in her stomach. "You know, I've been getting messages from Brenda asking me to call her. I've never called back. I don't know what to say. I'm over the anger. But I still don't like her much."

"I hear ya. She's in a hard place. I'm sure she's not making anything off the sale of the house. They owned it for only a year."

"Probably not. Maybe I should return her call."

Jess put her hand on Randi's. "Forgiveness is more powerful to the person who gives it than to the one who asks for it."

"Yeah, I've forgiven both of them. I'm just not crazy about being close to either one. Of course Cal's disappeared. Brenda must be really hurting."

"I imagine." Jess took the paper and tossed it in the trash.

"What did you do that for?"

"There are other houses. Besides, I want my best friend to come visit. I wouldn't want you staying away because of who lived there before me."

"I don't think I'd have a problem with that."

"No problem. Hey, tell me—why'd you go out with Jordan? I thought you were keeping a low profile with him."

"He's a nice guy."

"I noticed."

Jordan's comment about her being his second friend in town came to mind. Randi asked, "Are you interested?" They'd had an unwritten rule that if one of them was interested in dating a guy, the other would stay away from him.

"No. He's not my type. Although he does have that handsome actor, shoulder-length hair thing going for him."

Randi smiled. "Yeah, he does."

"So what's he like on a date? Details, girlfriend—I want details."

"First off, it wasn't a date. I wanted to thank him for saving my life."

"Oh, right. Fill me in on that one , too."

Randi laughed and shared, ever so briefly, about the two major events in her life the day before that involved a certain Jordan Lamont.

"Well, I must tell you, he did better than you and showed up for service today."

"Ugh. Don't remind me. I can't believe I overslept."

"It's your first date since Cal." Jess raised her finger to hold off Randi's protest. "It *was* a date, no matter what you say. He paid. How was that a reward for saving your life?"

Randi clamped her mouth shut and pouted.

"Gotcha. By the way, he's about to come in." Jess waved toward the sliding glass door.

Randi turned to see him holding a tall glass of tea in his hand. His hair was down, and his trusty rubber band was on his wrist. His appeal went so much further than that. Their ability to talk last night about deep and hurtful events in her life wound him tighter around her heart.

"Close your mouth. You're drooling," Jess whispered.

&

Jordan eased through the sliding glass door toward Miranda. "How sore are you?"

"Not too bad. The extra rest helped."

"Good. I'm sorry I tackled you so hard."

"Don't be."

Jess popped up. "I'm going to get another burger. Anyone else want one?"

"No, thanks."

"I'm fine," Jordan said, closing the distance between him and Miranda. "You haven't touched one of your burgers. I thought they were your favorite."

A nervous chuckle escaped her lips. "Were. Now I prefer steak."

"Ah." He sat down beside her at the table.

"Dena's happy with your design of her Web page. When can we spend some time working on a proposal for mine?"

"Soon." She took a huge bite of her hamburger. Jordan loved a woman who ate in front of a man. He'd had too many dates who would eat rabbit food in public, only to go home and eat something else. If they wanted a steak dinner, they should have ordered it. But, no, they were trying to impress. Instead it only turned him off. It was another thing he liked about Miranda. He really did like her real name more than her nickname. He supposed it had something to do with Randi sounding like a guy's name. Over the years, many people had mistaken his name also.

"I'm going on a photo shoot to the Sudan next week. How about when I get back?"

Her eyes wide, Miranda nodded, still chewing her burger.

"Hey, you two, come on out. It's time for volleyball."

She groaned. "Coming."

"Are you sure you're up for it?"

"If I don't start moving, I'll just be worse tomorrow."

"All right then. I believe we've been summoned." Jordan stood up and dumped his empty paper plate in the trash.

"You don't know the half of it. Have you ever played with these guys before?"

"I'm afraid I haven't. Why?"

"Well, I know how you feel about exercise. Let's just say you're going to be hurting worse than I am now."

He could feel the blood drain from his face.

She looped her arm around his. All the blood came rushing back. "Lead on."

An hour later, Jordan sat exhausted on the deck.

"You need to start running." Dena slapped a towel on the rail beside him.

"I see you're huffing and puffing."

"Yeah, but I'm twice your age."

"Touché." Miranda laughed. "He has a thing about exercise. It's not in his vocabulary."

"Yes, it is. I just choose to ignore it."

Everyone broke out in laughter. After tall glasses of ice water, most of the guests started leaving. Jordan gave Wayne a hand cleaning up, while the women went inside to work on the dishes.

"So how do you like Squabbin Bay?" Wayne asked.

"I like it." Jordan lifted a couple of paper plates that had blown off the railing.

"Are you looking forward to your photojournalism trip to the Sudan next week?"

"Yes. I hope to get a few things settled in the studio before I leave." This trip to the Sudan was just the kind of opportunity he'd hoped to get while working for Dena Russell Kearns.

"Dena says that area of the world is especially pretty but filled with civil unrest at the moment. Have you taken to heart what she's told you regarding safety measures?"

"Absolutely. She's been doing this for a while now."

"I'm just glad you're taking the trip and not her," Wayne said. "Not that I want anything bad to happen to you, but. . ."

Jordan chuckled. "If I had a wife, I wouldn't want her going either."

Wayne smiled. "I'm glad you understand." He shoved a smaller bag of garbage into the large green one he was holding. "Looks like I'll be running to the dump tomorrow morning."

"Now that's one reason I'm glad I'm living in town. I can at least put my trash cans out for pickup."

"It's taken me a bit to get used to. But for this view I don't mind."

Jordan turned and fixed his eyes upon the dark blue waters of the seascape. The ocean seemed calm and tranquil. He took in a deep breath and let it out slowly. "Yeah, I think I could get used to no trash removal for this view also."

"Hey, you two, what's taking so long?" Dena called from the sliding glass door.

"Just admiring the view, hon. We'll put these bags in my truck and be right in."

"Actually I have to be going. Thanks for the dinner, Dena. I'll see you in the morning at the studio." Jordan took the bag he was filling and carried it to the truck. A quick handshake with Wayne, and he was off.

In the rearview mirror, he could see Dena and Wayne's house. Inside sat the one person he'd love to spend more time with. But he'd taken off most of yesterday, and the pile of work to finish before he left town loomed in front of him.

Back at the studio, he started working right away. By ten he was feeling the lateness of the night before and went straight to bed.

His phone rang. "Hello?"

"Jordan, it's Randi. There's a stranger in the bushes in front of the studio."

"What?"

"I was driving by and saw someone."

"What would they be doing in the bushes?" His mind traveled to the equipment downstairs. "Call the police." He hung up the phone, slipped on his jeans, and tiptoed down the stairs.

eight

Randi had been so embarrassed for getting the entire town in an uproar after assuming she'd seen someone in the bushes. She'd kept herself hidden for the past week—which meant Jordan was now in the Sudan and away from her silly behavior.

"Hey, Randi," Charlie Cross greeted her as she walked into the post office. "Seen any bushes lately?"

"Hardy, har, har, Charlie. I saw something."

"Probably did—a coon or something. Don't mind the teasing. You did the right thing."

"I know."

Charlie held the door open for her, and she entered the post office. "Hello, Mabel. How are you?"

"Fine, fine. Folks still giving you a hard time about last week?"

"All in good fun," Randi admitted.

"Well, if you don't mind me saying so, I think you did the right thing. I heard Georgette Townsend the other day say things were looking mighty strange at some of the rental cottages."

Randi didn't want to get into a gossip session, so she kept quiet.

Didn't take long before Mabel had all the details out. "Too many strangers living in town these days. I think there're five right now."

Jordan would still be one, and possibly Dena. Although, having married Wayne, she's probably no longer one of the five. "I know of Jordan."

"He's no never mind. He works for Dena. It's the group of

64

folks renting the two cottages on Westwood Creek Road. I saw one at the festival, but none of the others came out."

"Well, that doesn't make them strange. Not everyone in town came out for the festival."

"True, but you'd think—oh, don't mind me. I don't know what to think. Georgette, she's the one that's all fired up about them. Not that she's called the police or anything. They haven't broken the law or nothing. They're just strangers and don't come into town much."

"Speaking of coming into town. . ." She needed to get Mabel redirected to the task at hand, or she'd be stuck here for an hour. "I need to mail these."

"Oh, dear, listen to me rattling on so." Mabel weighed the mail. "That will be four dollars and eighty cents, please."

Randi handed her a five and pocketed the change. With the mail done, she headed to her waitressing job. Oddly enough, she hadn't known of strangers moving into town. She wondered when that had happened and how she had missed it. Was Squabbin Bay actually growing?

Customers passed through quickly, tips were accumulating, and Randi felt good about the day.

"Hey, Randi, how you doing?" Jess plopped down at the counter.

"Good. How's your day?"

"Wonderful. I'm all excited. The paperwork has gone through with the state. We officially have a lobster fishing co-op."

"Woo-hoo! That's great news! What can I get you?"

"A banana split. I feel like celebrating."

"Coming right up." Randi topped off another customer's coffee then scooped up an oversized banana split for Jess. "Here you go. I'll be right back." Randi checked on her other customers and returned to Jess. "So what does this mean?"

"The goal is to get a better price for the lobster in order to stabilize the market somewhat. We're also working with the hatchery to bring in more fertilized lobsters to have their eggs hatched in the safety of the hatchery then later released to keep the numbers up."

"Well, look at you. That college education really paid off."

"You know, I never thought of having a business career in Squabbin Bay, but I'm really happy doing it. It's like I have the best of both worlds. I love business and all that's involved in that, but I also love the quietness of living in a small town. This way, I can have both."

"I'm proud of you, Jess."

"Thanks."

Randi ran off to assist a customer then returned again. "You know I'm happy with my work, but I feel something is missing."

"You mean Jordan."

"No." Randi smiled. "Not that."

"So you do miss him?"

"I'm afraid so. Please tell me how I can miss a guy I don't even know."

"What is it you feel you don't know about him?"

"Everything. I don't know who his parents are. I don't even know where he grew up." Randi took a cloth and wiped down the counter, removing the dishes and money first. "I wish I didn't have to work two jobs."

"Ah, I know what you mean. But apart from my stepmom, who do you know that doesn't?"

"Well, Pastor Russell doesn't."

"Okay, that's one. Who else?"

"I'll admit there aren't many, but wouldn't it be nice just to work one job?"

"Yeah, but that brings its own distractions, as well. I didn't work long in the corporate world, but it was long enough to know you can't trust anyone. Personally, I don't want to live like that."

Randi pulled the salt and pepper shakers out from under

the counter and started filling them. "I don't either, and I'm not saying I want to work in the corporate world, but I'd love to have one job support me, you know."

"Yeah, I know." Jess took a spoonful of ice cream. "Speaking of one job, look at Jordan. He's working two, as well. Have you heard from him?"

"No. We don't have that kind of relationship."

"You will. I can tell." Jess stirred her melting ice cream with a spoon then looked straight at Randi. Randi pulled her gaze away from her. "You love him, don't you?"

"Jessss." Randi spilled some salt onto the counter.

"Randi, number five is up," the short-order chef called from the kitchen through the half wall.

"I'm coming." Randi walked toward the pickup window.

"You and I will have to have a serious talk. How about tonight?"

"Can't." Randi passed Jess and brought the order to the table and checked with a few of the other customers before returning to the counter. "Tomorrow night I'm free."

"I'm not. I have a special meeting with the youth going on the mission trip." Jess had gotten involved with the youth group since she'd moved back to Squabbin Bay.

Randi hadn't felt so inclined. Her ministry revolved more around technology, and her contribution was working with kids like Digger to enable them to help the church. "You know, Jordan would have loved to go along on that."

"Yeah, but you're right. Parents would have been concerned. Maybe next year." Jess polished off the last of her ice cream. "That was yummy."

"Good—you deserved it."

"Speaking of the youth mission trip, how come you didn't volunteer?" Jess wiped her mouth with the paper napkin.

"I didn't have the funds, and I have a couple of clients who have scheduled a Web-page overhaul for that month."

"Ah. Well, maybe you can do it next year."

"Maybe." The thought of her and Jordan being on a mission trip together gave her a sense of joy. He obviously loved missions. The photo op he'd been sent on to the Sudan was for a Christian mission. Dena was going to do the job, but at the last minute she had asked Jordan if he'd take her place. She refocused on Jess's question. "How about Thursday morning?"

"Done. I'll meet you at your place after I come in from fishing."

Randi waved off Jess's attempt to pay for the banana split and paid for it herself from her tips. Fishing for lobsters wasn't Jess's only occupation. She knew her best friend was fishing for answers regarding Jordan.

Randi only wished she had them.

અ

At home, Jordan wiped off the African dust from his cameras and lenses—after a long and warm welcome from Duke, who'd been staying with Jess in his apartment. The purchase he made before moving to Squabbin Bay paid off. Each day he'd gone out with four cameras. One film, two digital SLRs, and another small digital for wide-angle shots if he couldn't frame a picture with the other three. He prayed that the pictures he'd taken—of civil unrest, matching the turbulent winds that kicked up the desert sands—would cause folks to pray more and give more to the various charities trying to help the Sudanese people. He knew the trip had been a life-changing experience for him. On the flight home, he'd decided that all profit from the pictures would go to various Christian missions working with these people.

Tomorrow he'd have to take the cameras completely apart and clean them. Tonight he needed to stay awake long enough to adjust back to his time zone. He'd been grateful for the opportunity, but he definitely liked his own country. He sat down at his computer and viewed the myriad of pictures he'd taken, stopping at the one of a militia gun to the head of a Sudanese woman, whom they claimed was a rebel. A knot squeezed tighter in his gut. If he hadn't been there, the woman would have lost her life. The child at her breast held no meaning to these men. What mattered to them was whether or not she was a rebel, and if so, she would be killed.

Jordan shook off the memory. "Thank You, Lord, that they didn't shoot her. Lord, continue to protect her and her child." He had never wanted to be a war correspondent–type photographer. War and crimes of passion were not his kind of picture. Sorrow and hurt were, and he could see the worries for this child and his future flick through the woman's eyes in a nanosecond.

He stared a bit longer at her brown eyes. Memories of Miranda's dark eyes flooded in. His mind drifted from one place to another. He closed his eyes and opened them slowly. He was home, safe, and forever changed. "Teach me, Lord, all You would have me learn."

Glancing at the clock, he lifted the phone and called Miranda. She answered on the second ring. "Hi, Miranda. It's me, Jordan."

"Hi, Jordan. When did you get back?"

"An hour ago." They talked for a few minutes; then he asked the question he'd called for. "Would you be up for a cup of hot cocoa and a stroll down at the point?"

She hesitated. "Sure."

His confidence soared.

"Let me finish up with this client. I could be ready in thirty minutes."

"All right. I'll pick you up in thirty." Jordan hung up the phone. Miranda was the first person he wanted to share his thoughts with. *Is she ready for that kind of relationship, Lord? I don't want to push her.*

He put Duke in the Jeep then drove to her house with a thermos full of hot cocoa and a cooler with some ice water. Hesitating, he rubbed his hands back and forth on the steering wheel then closed his eyes. "Lord, help me to be myself and not mess up."

"Talking to yourself?" Miranda stood beside the passenger door in a pair of jeans and a dark T-shirt. "Hey, Duke."

Duke woofed and lapped his jowls.

Jordan wanted to swoop her up into his arms and hug her. Instead he simply smiled. "Hey, there. It's good to see you."

"Same. So what's up?"

"I wanted to share with you my experiences in the Sudan."

She slid into the bucket seat beside him. "Cool. I want to hear all about it."

Jordan slipped the vehicle into gear and headed out to the point. "It was awesome but terrifying at the same time. The stories are brutal, but the mission work has been fruitful. They've put in wells, which completely changes a community."

They talked all the way to the point. "I don't think I'll ever be the same."

"There's something more, isn't there?"

"Yes. Let's go down to the beach first."

"All right."

He knew she was thinking it had to do with their relationship, which it didn't. But then again, maybe it really did. "I need to walk this out. Come on, boy. You need the exercise."

"And you don't like exercise."

He chuckled. "Sometimes a man just has to." They walked down to the shore's edge, leaving their shoes farther up the beach. Duke waddled behind, stopping every now and again to sniff at a clump of seaweed. "I had an encounter with the radical forces in Sudan. You're aware they'll kill a person who has converted from Islam to Christianity, right?"

She nodded.

"We were forced to stop at an impromptu checkpoint by radical forces. They questioned us at gunpoint and let us go when they discovered our journalism passes. At the same time, a woman was being taken away with her child. They said she was a rebel, and perhaps she was—I don't know. But deep down in my gut, I know that if I hadn't been there with all my cameras and the entire group with me, they would have killed her right there on the side of the road."

"Oh, my." Miranda reached out and placed her hand on his arm. "What happened?"

"I don't know. I pray she's safe, but I honestly don't know. Sometimes we just have to leave things in God's hands."

"Yes, you're right, but are you okay?"

"I think so. It was so raw and real. I know it is going to change me permanently in some ways. How, I'm not certain. I'm still in a bit of shell shock. If it hadn't happened on our last day, maybe I would have worked it through some more. But we were on our way to the airport."

"Another reason they probably didn't kill her."

"Quite possibly. There was a look in her eyes. . .I don't know. . .I can't describe it."

"What is it with you and eyes?"

"Huh?"

"Sorry. I didn't mean for it to come out that way. But ever since I met you, you've mentioned my eyes. And the one photo I found on the Internet done by you was of this old Native American woman, and in her eyes was a reflection of you. It was a great pic, but kinda strange."

Jordan smiled. "That's my great-grandmother. I was in college and won an award for that picture."

"Really. You're an Indian?"

"Fourth generation, if you count from my great-grandmother. That was a special day in celebration of our heritage. In truth, my great-grandmother lived in the city with my great-grandfather and then with my grandmother. My great-grandfather was a professor. Later he went into real estate. He was white. My grandmother is of a fair complexion, and my mother is even fairer. And, as you can see, there isn't much melanin in me. Well, except for this tan I picked up in the Sudan."

"Wow! You're Native American?" she repeated.

"One eighth, yes. Does it matter?"

"No, I just don't know much about you and your family."

Jordan rolled out a blanket he'd carried down on top of the cooler. Duke sat in the middle. Miranda sat on the opposite side. "I didn't spend much time with my Indian cousins. But once a year we would go to various tribal ceremonies. It was required as long as my great-grandmother was alive. I continued even after she died."

"I'm sorry. This took us off the subject you wanted to talk about."

"You know, it might be related. You mentioned my interest in eyes. I've always seen them as the window to one's soul. In the picture of my great-grandmother, my reflection was superimposed on the pupil. I actually could see myself, but the reflection wasn't clear, so I played with the image and placed myself in there. It was a comment on my great-grandmother's love for me, as well as my love for my heritage."

"There's so much we don't know about one another."

"Miranda, there are a lot of things. We haven't had the time." He wanted the time; he wanted to get to know her better. His life experiences flooded to the surface. All of a sudden, he wanted to share everything he'd learned and gone through in life, his relationship with God, his family.

Jordan reached over and took her hand. "Miranda, I want to be your friend."

"That's my problem," she said. "I want more."

Jordan's heart thudded in his chest. *Calm down. Count. One, two. . .*

"Jordan?"

nine

Randi tightened her grip on Jordan's hand. After what seemed like an eternity, he opened his eyes. "I do, too." He paused. "You were the first person I wanted to share my experiences with."

"I've missed our time together. Is it possible to be just friends?"

"I think your mother is right. Friendship is key to a healthy marriage." His eyes widened. "Not that. . .I mean. . . ," he stammered.

Randi let out a nervous giggle. "I understand."

"Miranda?" His voice calmed her. She liked the sound of her name coming from him. "And you're afraid to let me close because of what Cal did to you?"

She nodded.

"Come here." He opened his arms for her.

She hesitated for a moment then stepped over to him and leaned her head against his chest. Sweet relief washed over her like the waves brushing up against the shore. It felt good to be in Jordan's arms.

"I will make you a promise. I will not cheat on you. If our relationship is not right to pursue any longer, I promise to be up front with my feelings and concerns. Okay?"

"You can't know how you'll feel—"

He placed his finger on her lips. "I promise, Miranda. I want what is best for both of us."

She kissed the tip of his fingers. How did he know the right things to say? She wrapped her arms around him. For the first time in longer than she could remember, she felt at peace. Then she heard him pray.

"Father, be with us and guide us as we seek Your will for

our lives. Help us to keep You as our central focus even when we want to put ourselves or one another ahead of You."

"Amen." Randi pushed away from his embrace. "So tell me more about your trip to the Sudan. Did you capture any wildlife? Go on a safari?"

They talked for an hour until the air started to chill. "Would you like some hot chocolate?"

"Yes, but I really need to get home. I need to finish my client's Web page."

"Speaking of Web pages, when can we start working on mine?" Jordan got up from the blanket and extended his hand to help her up. He set the cooler to the side and lifted the blanket. Randi grabbed hold of the corners, and they shook it out together. Duke sat there and watched them. "Duke, get up. It's time to go."

Randi draped the folded blanket over her arm. "How about tomorrow afternoon after I get home from work? Can you have some photos ready for me by then?"

"Sure. Digital?"

"They're easier to work with, but we can scan prints."

"All right. I've been giving some thought to overall design and layout."

"Good. Visit a bunch of different photographers' Web sites and see what you like and what you don't. Then we'll have a better idea of a design just for you."

Jordan smiled.

"What?"

"I love the way you brighten up when you talk about your computer work. It's not the same as when you talk about waiting on tables." He propped the blanket on top of the cooler then picked up both.

"Waitressing is necessary to help pay my bills. Web designing, I hope, will grow enough to make a living. I'd love to work only one job."

He headed toward his vehicle. She and Duke followed.

"That's not very commonplace in this area, is it?"

"Nope. We're hardworking people, but I'd rather do my hard work in the Web designing."

"I hear ya. I can't wait until I earn enough to support a family."

Randi stopped. "How much do you believe you need to earn before you can have a family?"

"I'm figuring enough to support my wife and kids with full insurance. I don't have insurance for myself yet. Also, I'd like to buy an old Victorian house and renovate it as a wedding present."

"Sounds nice. But more than likely, you won't be getting married until you're forty-five."

He placed the cooler in the back of his Jeep. "Why? I want to provide well for my family. Is that too much to ask? I'm not asking to be the richest man in the world, but I do want certain things."

She raised her hands to his protest. "I'm not saying they are unreasonable, but shouldn't you think in terms of finding the right person then working with the Lord and her to provide the rest?"

He frowned. She hit a nerve and knew it. *Friendship might be as far as things could ever go between the two of us.* Money was something she worked for to provide the necessities. And, while she may want to plan for the future, she apparently figured she had plenty of time to do it.

"You're not into preparing for the future then." He hoisted the basset hound into the vehicle.

"Not really. I know I'll need to someday. But right now, I'm more concerned with earning enough to work only one job."

"I was raised to plan for the future."

"How so?"

"Both of my parents were very strict about preparing for college and encouraging me to be debt free within a year or two out of college so I could prepare for marriage."

"And are you prepared?"

"No, at least not where I'd hoped to be. My education is paid off, and I have a nest egg for purchasing a house, but it's tied up. I don't spend it."

"I have a hundred and fifteen dollars and twenty-six cents in my savings."

Jordan chuckled. "Do you tithe?" He turned on the engine and started off.

"Of course."

"Start tithing another ten percent and put it in your savings each week."

"I can't. I won't be able to pay my rent. Wait. I thought you didn't have much. I mean, didn't you say you didn't have a lot and couldn't afford your cell-phone bill?"

"I don't count my savings as money I can touch," Jordan said. "Once it is in there, it is no longer a part of my thinking for my daily use."

Maybe I have been too lax with my finances. "You're serious, aren't you?"

"Absolutely. That's why I have to have a certain income before I consider marriage."

Yup, just friends. "Wow! I don't know if I could live that way."

"Try it—you might like it."

"I'll think about it."

He pulled up to the curb in front of the small cottage she rented. Even Jess, she recalled, was thinking of buying rather than renting. *Have I been all wrong about my money, Lord? Should I have kept living at home and saved up to buy a house?* "Good night, Jordan, and thanks for the evening. It's—it's been interesting."

" 'Night."

≈

Jordan slapped the steering wheel. "Why did I have to bring up money? Our values are so dissimilar."

The night had gone well until he'd brought up his desire to be able to provide for a wife and family before he married. But she did have a point with regard to searching for the right woman. He didn't agree it had to be first. He could still save and plan for that day even before he met the right woman. *The problem is—is she the right woman?* If so, he was definitely not financially ready for her. And could they be right for one another when they differed so much on financial issues? "What do you think, Duke? Would Miranda and I be fighting constantly over where and when to spend the money? Or, in her case, why save?"

Duke laid his head on his paws and hiked up one of his eyebrows.

"Okay, maybe that's unfair to her. She did say she intended to save for the future—just not today."

And what was his nest egg? Just a few thousand dollars he'd hoped would be four times that amount by now.

Lord, I know my overplanning is a problem, and I'm trying to trust You; but if Miranda is to be my wife, I'm not ready for her. What can I offer her?

Jordan went to bed that night and woke with the same question recycling in his brain even as he arrived at work.

"Good morning, Jordan." Dena poured a cup of coffee from the coffeemaker in the back room of the studio. "How was your trip?"

"Good, but I need to clean my cameras."

Dena chuckled. "Goes with the territory. Can I see your proofs?"

"Sure." Jordan brought up the folder with the photographs he'd downloaded. "I'll need to go to your darkroom and develop these later." He plopped six film canisters on the counter.

"Film does have its advantages."

"Yes, but I got some great shots with the digital." He loaded the picture viewer on his laptop and left the chair for Dena to view.

"Wonderful. These are great." *Click, click* went the computer keys. "What's this? This is powerful, Jordan. Look at her eyes."

On the screen was the shot of the Sudanese woman and child. The next shot panned out, revealing the gun to her head.

"I don't mind admitting it was a terrifying experience."

"Praise the Lord you came back in one piece."

"Yes, but I keep praying for this woman. I don't know if she's still alive or if they've killed her."

Dena paused for a moment. "I have an idea. Let's put this photo on my Web site, credited to you, of course, but make it free to be broadcast all over the net, with a prayer request for her and her child."

"I'd love to, but I signed a waiver with the magazine for the mission that sent me. They have first rights on all pictures taken."

"Ah, I forgot about that clause. I've signed a few of those myself a time or two."

Jordan poured himself a cup of coffee and held it in his hands. "Dena, may I ask you a personal question?"

"Sure. What's on your mind?"

"When you married your first husband, had he saved for your future?"

"Bill?" Dena chuckled. "No, we were poor college students, and he was heading to grad school. It was basically hand-to-mouth our entire marriage. We did manage to take out a term life insurance policy on him once we started ministry, and that's what helped me buy my first studio with an apartment upstairs. Why do you ask?"

"My parents have ingrained in me that I should be able to provide for my wife and family before I get married. Even possibly have our house purchased before that."

"And you're nowhere near those goals?"

"Right. Don't get me wrong. You're paying me a fine salary, and to toss in the apartment saves me a bundle. But—"

"You couldn't provide for a family on your current income," she finished for him.

Jordan nodded. He'd been doing a lot more of that since meeting Miranda; it was her habit to nod instead of reply, and now he was doing it, too.

"Sit down." She patted the chair next to hers. "I didn't have extra until my children were grown. I took on assignments once they were in college. I was fortunate; I have a good eye and was in the right place at the right time. To me, that was divine intervention. It isn't because of what I did or didn't do. It was a matter of God's timing for my life. On the other hand, life got so full with all the traveling. I was forgetting my family. I wasn't really forgetting them, but I didn't spend much time with them. I've learned that having money is almost as difficult as not having money. But this isn't what you're dealing with right now, is it?"

"No, it's the goals I've set for myself. I'm wondering if I set them too high."

Dena smiled. "This is probably coming up because someone, namely Randi, has caught your attention."

"In part. On the other hand, it is something I've been dealing with the Lord about for quite a while. It's hard not to go by the plan. To let go and let God."

"God is a God of order, right?"

He nodded in agreement.

"And He's wired you to be precise with regard to finances. That means He'll work with your natural talent and challenge you to trust Him when the numbers might not add up."

"But how?" Jordan wiggled in his seat. "No, wait. That's not the right question. While I was in Africa, I decided to give the profits from the pictures to the Sudanese missionary work there."

Dena smiled.

"That's so unlike me. I tithe, I give, but I've never given up all I'm going to earn for something like that before. If I continue to do that, I'll never have enough to get married."

"And there is your real problem. You are trying to step out in faith, and yet your logical mind is telling you, you can't pay the bills if you do this, right?"

"Right." *I know all this, but I obviously need to be reminded.*

"I can't judge whether you've done the right thing by deciding to give those profits to that ministry. It is noble and truly sacrificial. But I can tell you from my own personal experience that when I've given in that way, God's met my needs in other ways. I have volunteered my time and profit for many events over the years, like the festival, and God's always supplied my needs. And, in most cases, He's given me more than I needed."

Jordan closed his eyes. "Trust and faith."

"Most things boil down to those two issues, don't they?" Dena placed her hand on his shoulder. "With regard to Randi, do the same. If it is God's will, He'll work out the details. If it isn't, He'll work that out, too."

"You're right. It's just that. . ."

"You love her—I know. I've seen that look before." Dena winked. "Now let's get to work."

"The day is a-wasting." Jordan stepped up to the counter and went to work on the studio's computer. They continued through the morning.

"Can I see your candids from the festival?" Dena asked a while later. "There wasn't time before you left."

"Sure." He pulled up the folder, and Dena went through his pictures.

"This girl is a cutie."

Jordan glanced over. "Yeah, I don't know who she is. No one picked up her picture at church after the festival."

"Well, that shot is a keeper. Can't sell it without a release form from the parents, but you could put a copy of it on your Web page. When is that going up?"

"Randi said we could work on it this afternoon."

"Great. Well, look—I'm meeting Wayne for lunch, and then

we'll be out for the next couple of days. We're going to Boston to visit the kids. Feel free to use the lab whenever you need to."

"Thanks. I'll probably go over there this evening."

"No problem. Call Jess and let her know. She's going to house-sit for us."

They said their good-byes, and Jordan glanced back at the picture of the girl with the toothless grin he'd taken in the hippo pool. She was cute, and the shot wasn't too bad either. He added it to his list of pictures for his Web page.

He answered the ringing telephone. "Hello?"

"Hey, Jordan, it's Randi. Can you come to my studio today rather than my coming there? Some time-sensitive items are due in before the end of the day, and the customer wants them on his Web site yesterday."

"That'll be fine. Should I bring some lunch?"

"Nah, I've already eaten. Bring your own if you like. Otherwise, I'm good."

"Okay, I'll see you later." Jordan gathered up his photographs, called in a take-out order from the Dockside Grill, and fetched his laptop and photo CDs, just in case he missed something.

"Duke, guard the fort. I'll be back shortly."

Duke raised his head inquiringly then settled his chin on the floor in resignation.

Jordan ran over to the grill and paid for his lunch. As he crossed the street toward the studio, he noticed a thin man peering in the studio's front-door window. "May I help you?" Jordan asked as he approached.

The man ignored him and walked back to his car. Jordan walked faster to catch up. "Can I help you?"

"No, thanks, I was just looking for my wife."

"Okay." Jordan turned to see the man drive away in a silver Volkswagen bug with out-of-state plates.

Back at the studio, he turned the sign around and posted his return by 3:00 p.m. He hoped his absence wouldn't mean any more loss of customers.

ten

Using the templates she had put together for other Web pages, Randi had the basic design of Jordan's done later that evening. The time would be in the graphics and giving an honest representation of Jordan and his work.

Jordan's homework for the night was to develop information on digital photography, his area of expertise. This would set his Web page apart from Dena's.

She crawled into bed much later than planned, but that was the way it happened from time to time. She was thankful she didn't have to go to work the following day.

Early the next morning, she went out for her five-mile run down by the point and came upon Jordan's Jeep. She searched the area but didn't see him. She continued running down the point to the marshy shoreline. There she found him, kneeling in muck with his camera aimed toward the sunrise. "You're nuts."

He turned and smiled then went back to his picture taking.

She wouldn't disturb him again. Thoughts of their second meeting flickered back in her mind. He'd been aiming his camera on a mother duck and her ducklings, and she'd messed up his shot. She picked up her pace and headed away from Jordan and his camera. After circling around and heading back toward home, she found him standing in the middle of the road, his pants soaked with mud and his arms across his chest. Duke looked out from the front seat, perfectly clean and definitely content.

"You do have a way of distracting a man."

"You were in the muck."

Jordan laughed. "Yeah, but it was a clean shot between the rocks in the harbor."

"It might be." Randi stopped jogging in place and stretched. "It's still nuts. You're going to have trouble getting that smell out of your jeans."

"They'll wash."

"They will, but they'll still smell for a while unless—"

"Unless what?" He inched closer to her. "Is there some secret ingredient to cleaning your clothes from the tidal marshes?"

"Most folks don't go mucking around in them without their hip boots. Those hose right down."

Jordan looked down at his shoes. "I might need to get a pair of those."

"If you're going to be playing in the muck, you will."

"All kidding aside, I'm wondering if you would like to have breakfast with me."

"Sure. Where?"

"My place. I'm going to try to wow you with my culinary skills."

"Do you have any?" Randi's eyes immediately widened in self-recrimination. She hadn't meant to be so flip with him.

"I can handle a few things. But I do have one ace up my sleeve over most men who don't know how to cook."

"What's that?" She inched toward him.

He leaned into her. His gentle voice tickled her senses. "You'll have to come and see."

Gooseflesh rippled down her spine. "All right. What time?"

"Give me forty minutes to clean up."

Randi stepped back and started back down the road. "I'll see you there. Remember—I eat well."

"That's one of the things I love about you."

She lost her footing momentarily but regained it. *Love—he said* love, *Lord.*

❧

Jordan made it back to his place in record time. He added a cup of vinegar to the washing machine. He didn't know what secret washing ingredient Miranda had in mind, but vinegar cut a lot of smells. Of course, he would have to rewash or else smell like a dill pickle for a few days. He took the fastest shower he'd ever taken and returned to the kitchen. He whipped up a batch of crepes then ran back to his room and finished dressing. He buttoned the last button on his shirt by the time she knocked on the back door.

"Wow! You clean up well."

He brushed the back of his teeth with his tongue for one final check. "You're not so bad yourself."

Miranda came in and walked to the kitchen area. "So what's the big surprise? Hey, Duke, how you doing, boy?"

Duke ambled over to her and nuzzled in for his free loving. Jordan wished he were in Duke's shoes. Jordan pulled back his hair and wrapped it behind his head. "Patience. It involves blueberries, but I still have to wash them."

"Blueberries are always good."

"And whipped cream."

"Even better." She sat down at the table. "I finished a basic layout for your Web page last night."

"Wonderful. I'll take a look at it after breakfast. Oh, I forgot to tell you—Dena loaded a picture I took of a little girl at the festival to her Web site."

"Really? How come?"

"She loved it. There's a copy of the print I blew up for the parents on display in the studio. No one claimed it, so I can only assume they don't attend the church."

"More than likely. Did Dena recognize her?"

"Nope. Maybe you'll have better luck."

"I might, but I'm getting old enough that I don't know all the grammar school–age kids."

Jordan pulled out his crepe pan.

"Crepes? You know how to make crepes?"

"Oui. It was one of the things I learned in French class. I think it might have been the only day I paid attention actually."

"You—I can't believe it." She leaned on her elbows. "Were you a good student in school?"

"Fair. I didn't care much for school. I liked art and some of my other classes, but I just did what was required to get through. In college, I discovered I had to buckle down and study if I was going to graduate." He removed the plastic film he'd placed over the batter earlier. "Are you a big crepe-eater?"

"If they're stuffed, four, please."

"Yes, they'll be filled with whipped cream and blueberries." Randi licked her lips and closed her eyes. "Sounds heavenly."

Jordan turned back to the stove. "So what are your plans for the day?"

"Work. What about you?"

"Same. I have some film developing I need to do at Dena's. I'd hoped to do it last night; but I called Jess too late, and she'd already retired for the evening. I hope she's not working too hard."

"With regard to Jess, she'll be okay once the co-op is launched. Are the pictures of the Sudan?"

"Yeah, I shot a few rolls of film."

Jordan dipped the pan into the batter then flipped it over and placed it on the warm burner. Moments later, the crepe was ready to be turned over. He repeated the process.

"You're really good at this."

"It's the pan. It is amazing what happens with the right equipment."

A brisk knock on the front door of the studio rapped in his ears. Jordan glanced up at the clock. "Miranda, would you keep making the crepes while I take care of the customer?"

"Sure."

Jordan went to the front door and opened it. "May I help you?"

"I'm sorry to barge in like this, but that picture in the window. . . That's—that's my daughter. Where did you get it?"

Jordan glanced over at the little girl sitting in the hippo's mouth. He had it displayed with several other shots of the children from the festival. "I took it at the festival. Would you like it?"

"Yes, please." The woman's red hair overflowed her decorative scarf.

"No problem. It's on a mat but not framed yet."

"It's fine just the way it is."

Jordan reached over and pulled the picture from the window. "Here you go."

"How much do I owe you?"

"Nothing. Consider it a gift from Community Church."

"Thank you."

"Have a nice day."

As he watched the woman scurry off, Jordan remembered her as the same woman who had come in during the festival for one-hour film developing.

"What was that all about?" Randi asked as he entered the kitchen.

"Remember the collage of photos I put together of the festival and hung in the studio window?"

Miranda nodded.

"A mother saw her daughter and wanted it."

"She couldn't wait until you were open?"

"She's always on the run. She might be hyper—who knows? Now how are you doing?"

"Just about finished cooking up all the batter."

"Great. I'll make some blintzes for later."

"Blintzes?"

"Rolled-up crepes stuffed with cream cheese and other things. You make them ahead of time and freeze them."

"Hmm. Just how many French classes did you take?"

"Actually, blintzes are Yiddish."

"Hebrew class?"

"Nope, a neighbor." Jordan smiled. He relieved Miranda of

her duties and finished making the crepes, filling them with whipped cream and blueberries and then sprinkling some powdered sugar over the tops.

Jordan set the plates on the table and joined her. He grasped her hand. "Father, direct us in our relationship and lead us in Your design for our lives. In Jesus' name, amen."

"Amen." Miranda took her fork and cut off a large piece. She sighed with pleasure. "These are excellent. You can cook breakfast for me anytime."

Jordan's mind sprinted to the future, to a vision of the two of them married, living happily with one another, and him making breakfast for them and their children. Jordan opened his mouth and filled it to avoid sharing his heart and dreams with Miranda at this time. He didn't want to scare her again.

eleven

"Randi!"

Randi spun around at the sound of her name. Her spine stiffened. The subject of many sleepless nights and far too many hours on her knees appeared in all her blond, blue-eyed beauty. Randi nodded in acknowledgment then turned back in the direction she had been going.

"Randi, please," Brenda pleaded.

It had been well over a year since she and Cal had been married. Randi even told Jess she'd forgiven Brenda, but. . .

Randi came to a halt. She decided to face the backstabbing. . .

Forgive me, Lord. Help me. "What do you want, Brenda?"

"I want"—Brenda's eyes started to water. She hoisted the six-month-old child higher on her hip—"I want to apologize. It was wrong for me to date Cal while you two were still engaged. I knew it, but I ignored the truth and walked right into a horrible situation."

Randi shut her eyes for a moment then opened them, counting, *One, two, three.* "I forgave you a long time ago."

"Yeah, right. Look—I admit I was wrong. I didn't mean to hurt ya. It just happened. And look where it got me. At least you can be thankful you're not the one with a child and no husband."

"Brenda, I'm sorry Cal ran off on you, but what does that have to do with me?"

"Nothing. Everything. . .I don't know. Cal always blamed me for breaking you two up."

Randi shook her head. "Cal likes to blame others for his actions. That isn't to say you didn't play a part in his affair, but he shouldn't be blaming you. He was the one engaged." It felt good to say those words out loud.

"Yeah, my mother says if he walked out on you, he was more than likely going to walk out on me, too. I didn't believe her, but she was right."

"What are you going to do?"

"We hired a lawyer to track him down for child support, but the lawyer said not to hold out for much. He said even if they find him and require him to pay the child support, he still might not pay. Knowing Cal, he won't."

Randi's heart went out to Brenda. "How are you going to support yourself and the baby?"

"Mom's going to watch Tyler."

Randi's heart cinched. That was the name she and Cal had picked out for their first son.

"I'm going to work part-time and finish my college degree. Dad's going to help me with tuition and stuff. After a couple of years, I should be able to provide for Tyler and myself."

"Your folks live near Portland now, right?"

"Yeah, Daddy's working for the hospital there." She shifted Tyler. He had Cal's eyes. "I'm sorry, but life has bitten me—"

"Brenda, the Lord will help you," Randi said, cutting her off. She'd felt many times as if Brenda had gotten what she deserved, but the child didn't deserve a father who had abandoned him. Admittedly, at this very moment, Randi realized her "forgiveness" of Brenda and Cal was not complete. *Lord, forgive me.*

Brenda snickered. "God helps those who help themselves. And so help me, if I ever get my hands on Cal, I'll—"

"I'll be praying for you."

"You know, that's the problem Cal had with you, all that high and mighty stuff. I'm no saint, but at least I don't believe I can't do anything in life, that I live at the whim of God."

"It isn't at God's whim. It is a matter of submission, giving everything back to the Lord and trusting Him."

"Where was your God when Cal was cheating on you?"

Randi wondered why all this anger was coming at her

when Brenda had started out with an apology. "Cal cheating on me was not God's doing. God got me through, and I'm a stronger person now. Bad things happen in this world, Brenda. It's how we choose to live with those bad experiences that make or break us as human beings."

"You really believe all that stuff we learned in youth group with Mr. Kearns, huh?"

"Yup. And, trust me, it's helped me deal with you and Cal going behind my back."

"I wasn't the only one."

"I know." *Stick the knife in deeper. Lord, I don't understand why I'm going through this conversation with Brenda. She isn't even repentant. Not really.*

"You do? Cal said you didn't have a clue."

"As I look back now, I can see all the lies. But Cal was right—I didn't know then, or how many other women there were. I chose to overlook his lies and believe him in spite of what was happening around me." *No wonder I have trouble trusting Jordan.*

The baby started to cry.

Randi looked down at him. "Is something wrong?"

"He's hungry. I need to feed him." She glanced at her son. "Randi, I know I've been saying this all wrong. I am sorry for what happened between me and Cal and what it did to you. But I love my son. How could it have been so wrong?"

Randi took in a deep breath then let it out slowly. "Come on inside and you can feed Tyler."

"Are you sure?"

"Yeah, come on in." Randi let the one person in the world she despised most into her cottage, allowing the Lord to crumble the wall she'd built up for so long. She felt sorry for the woman and her child and knew they needed to get acquainted with Jesus. "Iced tea?"

"Sure, thanks." Brenda's knees shook as she sat down on the sofa.

Randi went to the kitchen then returned in time to see the baby nursing hungrily. "Here you go."

Brenda knitted her eyebrows together and peered at Randi. "Why are you being so nice?"

⋟

Jordan's Web page was fully designed and operating in three days. Miranda had done a wonderful job. She also included a blog for him to post pictures for people to comment on. The little girl with the great smile and no front teeth was the first photo he put on his blog. Today he noticed Randi had added a couple, as well. The work at the studio crawled along. Apart from customers coming in to have their pictures developed, they had no other studio work. Dena said it would pick up in the fall with school pictures. Jordan hoped she was right. He knew what came in, he knew his salary, and the two weren't that far apart. He set up an easel in the rear corner of the studio to work on between customers.

The crab-shack wharf was taking shape on canvas. He decided to go with high tide and reflect the building in the water below. He dabbed the titanium white and added a touch of cobalt blue and left the colors unmixed on his brush. With a careful hand, he dotted the water below.

The bell over the door chimed. Jordan turned to see a man with short, cropped, black hair and a form-fitting T-shirt and jeans walk in. "Can I help you?"

"Yeah." He inhaled a deep pull on a cigarette and breathed out the smoke. "Wife said you took this." He held up a photo of a young boy playing in the hippo pool.

"Yes, sir. Would you mind putting your cigarette outside?"

He took another pull and stepped outside to place his cigarette in a planter box. "I was wondering if you could make copies."

"Sure can. What do you need?"

The man went over the various photographs Jordan had taken of his son then placed an order. "I'd like these by tomorrow. Is that possible?"

"I can have them ready in an hour."

"Really? Awesome. I'll be back."

Jordan processed the man's order. The phone rang. "Hello?"

"Hi, Jordan, it's Dena. I'm wondering if you're up for another trip? Jamie Stewart had to cancel at the last minute, and I have family plans. I'll understand if you can't."

"When?"

"You need to leave on Friday night and fly out of Boston or possibly pick up a flight from Bangor. It's a three-day shoot in Niagara. You could drive if you want."

"No problem."

"There's one more thing. Jamie was taking an assistant because of the multiple shots required. Do you know of anyone who could go at such short notice?"

His mind flickered to Miranda. "No, I'm afraid not."

"All right. I'm sure you can handle it by yourself. You know what? Fly—don't drive. You'll be exhausted at the end, and flying home will feel much better."

"Yeah, but I'll still have a six-hour drive from Boston."

"True, but you could spend the night there. Your old roommates or parents could put you up, right?"

"More than likely. Don't worry, Dena. I'll take care of it." *I could use a visit with my folks.* "Oh, by the way, I had the first return customer from the candids I took at the festival."

"Excellent. You only charged for the prints, right?"

"Yes. We've discussed this before." He was beginning to understand small town logic, but it still bothered him not to make a profit on those prints. Then again, he'd had a lot of hits from the picture of the toothless-grinning girl on the Internet, and that was another freebie. Comments to his blog were along the lines of "What a beautiful smile," "Gotta love those freckles," and so on. A couple even inquired to know the child's name. He was thankful he didn't know and wrote back accordingly. Whether he'd received any orders because of that shot, he didn't know. But a few pictures had been requested from some of his previous work.

"Jordan, I'm sorry. I know this is a hard adjustment, but you're going to have to trust me on this."

"Dena, I do trust you. And I'm beginning to see the logic, although I'm not sure how it will all work out."

"It'll work out. Okay, I have to run. Contact me when you return."

Jordan gave his salutations then tapped out Miranda's phone number and reached her answering machine. "Hey, Miranda, it's Jordan. I'm afraid I can't make our dinner date Friday night. Dena's asked me to fill in for someone on a job. I'm going to Niagara." He glanced up at the calendar. "I'll see you in a week."

Jordan arranged for Jess to take care of his dog while he was gone. Duke enjoyed being on the water after spending a week with Jess during his trip to the Sudan. Jordan went back to his painting of the crab shack. He dipped his brush into the linseed oil and then a tiny dab of cerulean blue.

The jarring sound of screeching brakes, followed by the thump of one car hitting another, sent him running from his easel and out to the street.

twelve

Randi eased out a pent-up breath. "Brenda, I'm not all that nice. But God's been working on me and my anger toward you and Cal. Jesus loves you, and I'm called to love as He loves. I'm not a saint, and I can't do it on my own. But I do have compassion for you and Tyler. . .even Cal. He's missing out on his relationship with his son."

"I can't believe I fell for his lies."

Randi let out a nervous chuckle. "I'm with you there. I'm sorry he walked out on you."

Brenda sniffled. "He said I wasn't you."

"Brenda, you can't judge yourself from what Cal said. And you certainly can't judge yourself from me. The Bible tells us how God believes we're all wonderfully made and of His redeeming love for us. No matter what happened, He still loves you."

"How?"

"That's kind of a mystery to all of us. But we have His Word, and we have His actions—sending His Son to die for us—that proves He does love us and forgive us."

"I'm scared, Randi. I don't want to live with my parents, but I have no other choice. I can't allow Tyler to suffer for my mistakes."

Randi thought for a moment. "You know, your love for Tyler is like God's love for us. Your parents' love for you is the same. They warned you about your relationship with Cal, but they are allowing you to come back home, to provide for you and your child, even though you didn't listen to their counsel. Isn't that how God deals with all of us?"

Brenda wiped the tears from her cheeks and looked down

at her nursing son then back at Randi. "I knew if I came to you, you would help me sort this out. All this Jesus and God stuff is really real to you, isn't it?"

"Yup."

"Just like Mr. Kearns."

Randi nodded.

"I should have listened to him about that sex before marriage stuff. I thought he was so. . .well, I won't say it. But I really thought he had a few marbles loose just 'cause he had to raise Jess on his own. Now I'm in the same boat. Oh, I married Cal after I was pregnant, but he left me, just like Jess's real mom left her."

"They will be helpful people for you to talk with about raising Tyler without a father."

"I suppose. I just don't know if I can go through all that Jesus stuff. I mean, I'm glad He's real for you and all that, but I'm still not sure He can do anything for me."

Randi rubbed her hands together for a moment. "Pray, Brenda."

"I'll think about it."

Tyler slurped and rolled back his eyes. A knot tightened in Randi's stomach. The longing for her own child increased. She and Cal had planned on having children right away. Then her mind kicked back to something Jordan had said about children and how he wanted some. But not until he and his wife could afford them. She glanced back at Brenda. "Thinking things through and praying are the best things you can do."

"I didn't mean to stay so long." Brenda caressed Tyler's soft brown hair. "I'm leaving town today, and I've been trying to speak with you for so long."

"Why?"

"To apologize."

Randi nodded. "I realize that, but you've said you were sorry before. Why do you suppose you had such an urgent need to speak with me before you left town?"

Brenda turned away. "Because I tried to take Cal away from you," she muttered.

Randi already knew that from the gossip of others and even from what Brenda had said earlier, but it was good for her confess it. "You're on the road to recovering your faith, Brenda. You do believe in Jesus. You're just afraid to surrender your life to Him."

"I never wanted to live in Africa."

Randi chuckled. "Not everyone is called to be a missionary and go to Africa."

"I know but. . .oh, I don't know. It sure felt good to party and. . .well, you know."

Actually I don't. Thank You, Lord, for giving me the strength to resist Cal. "If sin didn't feel good from time to time, how would it be tempting?"

Brenda chuckled for the first time. "You sound like Mr. Kearns."

Randi smiled. "Yeah, I suppose I do. But it is still the truth."

"Yeah. I've gotten myself into quite a mess. But I don't want that for Tyler."

"Go to your parents," Randi said. "Do what you need to do to provide for your son, but get right with the Lord, Brenda. Nothing else will get you through some of the long hard days you have ahead of you. And, trust me, you'll be tempted to fall for the first guy who wants to provide for you and your son. Don't. Fall for the man the Lord will provide for you."

"Didn't you think Cal was that man for you?"

"Yes, but I've learned since that I wasn't trusting the Lord. I was just assuming Cal was the guy because that's what I thought I wanted back then. I don't now."

"No, I've seen you with the new photographer. He's pretty hot."

Randi's cheeks flamed. "Yes, he is."

"Do you like all that hair?"

She remembered his hair tickling her arm as he kissed the back of her hand. And then again when he'd worn it down at breakfast. "Yes, oddly enough I do. It fits him."

"That's so weird. Cal's is so short."

Randi hadn't made the comparison. Was she attracted to Jordan because he was so different from Cal?

Tyler finished nursing. An awkward, silent pause passed between them. Randi stood and walked to the window. From her cottage window, she could see the harbor. In the street below, people were running toward the center of town.

"Something's happening."

⁂

Jordan sat on the curb, paintbrush still in hand. He watched as the volunteer firemen used the "jaws of life" to remove a man trapped in his car.

"How come you aren't photographing this?" a crusty old fisherman called out from the crowd.

"Huh?" It had never entered his mind to grab his camera. If it had been a year ago, instinct would have taken over, and he would have grabbed the camera and cell phone. He would have been calling a major newspaper in the Boston region as he took the picture and then working his way down the list until one of the newspapers wanted his shots. With Dena working as his agent and with the more laid-back routine of living in down-eastern Maine, he realized he was more concerned with the individual who was trapped in the car than earning some money from someone else's misery. Not that he'd ever been that kind of photographer. But income was income, and generally he took any opportunity he could get.

"Ain't ya workin' for the newspaper?"

"Nope."

"Bet they'd pay to have a picture of this. That man in the car there is someone well-known in these parts."

"Thanks, but I'd rather be praying for his safety."

"Ah, prayer ain't a bad thing."

Jordan smiled and stood up from the curb. The volunteers worked methodically, cutting the car door and using the "jaws of life" to lift the roof high enough to pull the victim out. The driver of the car had run into the back end of a freight truck with a hydraulic lift on the rear, crushing the roof.

The bloody driver moaned. Jordan lifted another prayer for him, as he had been doing since seeing the wreck ten minutes ago. Jordan looked back at the truck then the car and noted how fortunate the driver was to be alive.

"Jordan, what's happening?" Miranda came running up, followed by a woman with a baby.

He held out his arm, and she drew close in his embrace. He sniffed her hair and felt ever so grateful she was safe. He explained what had happened. Miranda peered at the car.

The woman with the child gasped. "Oh, no!"

"Who is it?" Jordan asked.

Miranda left his embrace and steadied the woman. Jordan followed suit and took the baby from her arms. "That's Cal's father, Mike Collins, in the wreck. This," she told Jordan, nodding toward Brenda, "is Cal's wife and child."

"Cal, as in—" He cut off his question. This was no time to ask hows or whys.

"I need to call my parents," Brenda said.

Jordan reached for his cell phone then remembered he no longer had one. "You can use the phone in the studio."

Miranda led Brenda back to the studio. Jordan held the little boy in his arms and followed behind them. "Hey, there, little one, I'm Jordan. Who are you?"

The baby greeted him with a drooling grin.

"His name is Tyler," Miranda said as she opened the door for Brenda to go in.

"Phone's on the counter." Jordan turned back to the child. "Hey, there, Tyler. Would you like to play with a ball?"

The baby thumped Jordan's chest with his tiny fists. "I'll take that as a yes." Jordan put him on the carpeted area and pulled out a box of toys they kept on hand for children while they set up to take their photos. He glanced away and saw Brenda was on the phone. "What's going on?"

"I'll explain later."

"Okay."

"Is he alive?" Miranda asked.

"Yes, he's fortunate," Jordan replied. "There's a lot of blood, but there always is with a head wound. The firemen were on the scene within a few minutes."

"Good."

He had a thousand questions for Miranda, and looking at Brenda and Tyler he knew something had been transpiring between the two of them. But he'd wait. He'd give her the time she needed to tell him what was going on and why they were in one another's company. He took it as a sign that Miranda was moving on from the hurts of the past, giving him more hope for their future. Yes, she was going to be his wife one day; she just didn't know it yet. And he'd learned long ago not to tell a woman that before it was time. Back in college, a friend of his told a gal on their first date that they would marry one day. She ran away from him faster than a rocket lifts off from Cape Canaveral.

He picked up his camera and focused on Tyler. He was a handsome child. *Click.* He took a shot. *Click.* And another. Just then, Duke edged his nose around the doorway at the stairs to his apartment. Jordan held up his hand. Duke sat down and waited.

Brenda hung up the phone. "Mom's going to call Mrs. Collins and let her know about the accident. Do you think he'll be all right? Should I go to the hospital?"

Jordan thought it odd she was asking Miranda for help.

"I don't know," Miranda said.

"How are you?" Jordan asked. Perhaps if he understood

what Brenda's thoughts were at the moment, he could better understand what to suggest.

"Freaked out. Mom said he was probably coming to take Tyler away from me."

"Why?"

"Ever since Cal left they've been trying to get custody of Tyler. They say I can't support him. That's another reason I'm going to my parents' house."

"Why don't you have a seat? Can I get you something? A cup of tea?" Jordan offered.

"No, no, I'm fine. I've imposed long enough. Bye, Randi, and I'll think about what you said."

"Bye. And I'll be praying for you."

"Thanks." Brenda picked up Tyler and headed out of the studio then turned around. "And thanks for the use of the phone."

Then she was gone. They stood there for a moment in silence. The ambulance siren signaled its departure. Jordan rubbed the back of his neck. "What's going on?"

"She came by to apologize."

He edged up beside her. "How are you?"

ॐ

Randi sighed. "In the words of Brenda, 'freaked out.' I'm glad she's moving in with her parents. I was able to share about the Lord with her, and, for the first time, I no longer have that bitter taste in my mouth when I think about her and Cal. I'm sorry it happened, but in the end I'm over being hurt by his actions." She glanced out the window at the wrecked vehicle then back to Jordan.

"Do you think Cal's father was going to take the baby?" Jordan asked.

"It's possible. Cal's family has done fairly well. Consequently they kinda live by their own rules—which I should have seen ages ago but didn't. I guess I was so taken by the fact that Cal said he loved me that I overlooked a lot of things, including how his parents spoiled him. I don't think they'd be the right people to raise Tyler."

"What about Brenda?"

"I think she's grown up a lot since she became a mother. If you had asked me before she had the baby, I would have said no way. Today I think she's on the right track. It would be better if she trusted the Lord, but that's between her and God to work out."

"I've missed you." Jordan stepped closer to her.

Randi's legs felt like Jell-O. "It's only been a couple of hours, if that."

"I know." He wrapped his arms around her. "I still missed you."

With all the strength she could muster, she stepped out of his embrace. "Do you think this is wise?" Duke came over and sat on her foot as if anchoring her to stay put.

"Honey, I love you. Seeing that man in the car, my first thought was, I'm glad it wasn't you. I didn't think about getting my camera. . .nothing but you. Are you ready to be more than friends?"

Randi closed her eyes. *He confessed his love; should I?* She opened her eyes and slowly focused on the sparkling hazel of Jordan's. "I want to."

Jordan beamed. "Good. Then may I kiss you?"

Prickles of gooseflesh rose up and down her spine. She took a half step toward him and traced his lips with her finger. He kissed it gently. "Yes," she whispered.

He leaned over, and Randi closed her eyes.

"Jordan?" The front door of the studio slammed open.

Randi's eyes flung open.

"Randi?" Jess stood there with her hands on her hips. "Did I . . . ?" Her words trailed off. "Sorry," Jess mumbled. She turned and marched out of the studio.

"What was that all about?" Randi asked.

"I don't know, but her timing leaves a lot to be desired."

Maybe. The moment had passed. Randi slipped out of Jordan's embrace.

"Miranda?"

"We should see what Jess wants."

"Uh, sure. Whatever you say." Jordan went after Jess.

Randi tried to regain her footing. She knelt down and patted Duke. Was she really ready to involve herself with that level of commitment to Jordan? She still didn't know him all that well. Could she truly trust him? What were his parents like? An image of Jordan and her in their own home with children in the living room and the two of them preparing breakfast in the kitchen flickered through her mind.

Is he the one?

thirteen

Jordan packed his bags and flew out to Niagara Falls the next day. Jess's interruption had ended the kiss before it happened. Miranda pulled out of the studio faster than an old-fashioned camera flash burning the powder in the trough. And to be confronted by lovers strolling arm-in-arm all over Niagara on the Canadian side of the falls just reminded him of what they didn't have.

He was still puzzling over this when he flew back to Boston three days later. He'd thought of calling Miranda at least a hundred times, but he never got up the nerve. The fact that he no longer had a cell phone made it even more problematic. And she couldn't call him, with no number where she could reach him. But something still didn't feel right. Should he call? Or should he wait patiently for Miranda to be over the pain Cal had caused her?

On the other hand, Brenda's uninvited visit and Miranda's reaction to it indicated she was ready to move on. But then again, she had left the studio before he returned with Jess. This circular thinking was getting him nowhere. He took the T and walked up the hill to his parents' home. They lived a few blocks from Fenway Park. Cars lined the streets. *The Red Sox must be playing tonight.* A person could watch the game from his parents' roof.

He took the steps two at a time and knocked. His mother answered. She looked good, and her smile sent a wave of peace through him. "Hey, Mom."

She pulled him into a bear hug. "It's good to see you, Jordan. We've missed you."

"I've missed you, too. What are you cooking? It smells

103

good." He stepped into the front hall.

"New England boiled dinner." She closed the door behind them. The coolness of the air-conditioning felt wonderful.

"My favorite."

She winked. "I know. But your father enjoys it, too."

"Where is he?"

"Down in the basement. Go put your bag in your room. I'll tell him you're home."

"Thanks." He hadn't lived at home for years. It seemed strange that his folks still called it his room, especially since it had become his mother's craft room. But there in the corner sat the twin bed and dresser he had used since he was two years old. He glanced at the table and looked over her newest scrapbook. It held pictures of him and his siblings when they were young. He thumbed through the beautiful pages she had designed and laid out. His mind filled with childhood memories, page after page.

"Jordan!" his father's voice boomed through the room. "Good to see you, son."

"Good to be home, Dad."

"So you're working more with this Dena Russell?"

"Yup, I have a nice, steady income now."

"Wonderful. Aren't those"—he pointed to the scrapbooks— "great?"

"Yes, she's done an incredible job."

"I think so, but, then again, I didn't mind just looking at the pictures in the plastic sleeves. Can you tell me why the pictures from the sixties are turning color?"

"It was the process they used back then. You can have them scanned and restored. I can do it for you if you'd like."

"That would be wonderful. Your mom's had duplicates made of most of the photographs before she puts them in the books. Not to mention duplicates so each of you kids can have your own copies."

"You mean I'll get to have these one day?"

"Absolutely. They'll be good to have especially when you have children. On the other hand, they'll be even better to have for me to show my grandchildren."

"First, I need a wife."

"That would be helpful. So tell me more about this gal in Maine. Randi, I think her name is, isn't it?"

Jordan took in a deep pull of air. "Yeah, it's Randi. Miranda is her full name. I love her—I really do—but she's been hurt by a fiancé who ran around on her. At least she found out before they married, but it still has her in a tailspin of sorts. I know she doesn't fully trust me."

"Trust develops over time, son. Give her a chance. She'll come around if she's the one the Lord has in mind for you."

"I think she is, Dad. And I'm trying to be patient."

"But that's not really your strong suit, except with photography."

Jordan chuckled. "Yeah, except with photography. So what are you working on in the basement?"

"I've taken up a new hobby," his dad said. "I'm learning how to make stained glass."

"Wow! How are your fingers?"

"Ha, ha. I've only nicked 'em a couple of times. Cutting the glass is the easy part. Laying out the design and using the copper foiling is tough, but I'm starting to get the hang of it. After that, I'll work on learning how to use the lead. The copper foil, though, is your mother's favorite."

Jordan was happy his parents found hobbies to keep them busy. He knew retirement was only a few years away for them, and he loved the idea that they kept active. "Lead on—I'd love to see what you've done."

As they passed by the kitchen, his mother called out, "Don't stay down there too long! Supper will be ready in fifteen minutes."

"Not a problem, Mom. I'm starved."

"You won't have to call me twice for dinner," his father

added with a smile.

Jordan quieted the laughter that bubbled up inside him. Once his father was in the basement, it took a lot of prodding on his mother's part to get him to come up for dinner.

They rounded the corner, and both ducked as they went down the narrow basement stairs. One thing about old houses in the Boston area—they generally were made in the 1800s when stairways were put in some of the tightest spots of a house. Jordan lifted his hand and reached out to the carrying beam that had beaned him more times than not when he was growing up and moving too quickly.

"Tell me more about Miranda. What does she do? Look like? And why do you love her?"

Nothing like his father to get to the heart of the matter. "She's beautiful—inside and out. She has these wonderful dark gray eyes."

"Like your great-grandmother's?"

"Yeah."

"Interesting. Do you have a picture?"

"On my laptop. I'll show you after dinner."

"I'd love to see your work. Have you looked into the real estate in Squabbin Bay?"

Jordan chuckled. "I haven't, but I guess you have?"

"Absolutely. The market hasn't moved much in years up there. The area seems to be just far enough away from the general tourism routes that it is still secluded and underdeveloped."

They continued talking until his mother called them for dinner. Jordan enjoyed the time with his parents. He found it helped to settle him down, to continue being patient with Miranda.

੨

Driven by distraction, Randi paced back and forth in her cottage. Jordan hadn't come home from his Niagara trip yet. Jess had said he might spend the night in Boston, but she had no contact information for him. "E-mail! Why didn't I think of that before?" She thumped her head and sat down at her desk.

Pulling up Jordan's contact information, she typed his e-mail address into a new mail window then proceeded to type.

"*Dear Jordan. . .*" She paused. "Dear" seemed too formal. She hit the delete key and held it down until all the letters were erased then tried again. "*Hi, Jordan. . .*" Her fingers paused again on the keys. Why was it so hard to type a simple e-mail? What did she want to say anyway? "*I miss you.*"

"*I'm sorry I ran out of the studio when Jess showed up.*"

Nah, that wouldn't do. Her desire for the kiss had turned the instant Jess walked in on them. All the old fears resurfaced. There was no question she was attracted to Jordan, and the attraction went way beyond his looks. She loved their time together, loved being able to talk so openly with him. But she was afraid of being vulnerable once again. A few days ago, she was confident in moving on. Today she still was. . . . But thinking back on the near kiss. . .as much as she wanted it. . . Fear wrapped its ugly head around her logic.

Randi deleted the e-mail. She should wait until they could speak one-on-one.

The computer flashed that she had incoming e-mail. It was from Jordan. She smiled and opened it.

Hi, Miranda,

This is just a quick e-mail to let you know I'll be back in town tomorrow evening. I'm wondering if we can go out to dinner. Please let me know. Also I'll be bringing up some of my earlier work. I thought we might be able to put some of the photos on my Web site and others in stock-photo archives.

See you soon.

Jordan

Randi reread the e-mail. Then she reacquainted herself with some of the various Web pages that kept stock-photo archives and the costs for those services and checked into their search capabilities. She smiled to herself, thinking about how this stuff made her parents' heads spin. They didn't understand the computer world and her career. They knew it could be a great benefit for those who used it regularly; they just didn't happen to be such people. She wondered if Jordan's folks kept up with computer technology. Even as techno savvy as she tried to keep herself, the industry kept growing at a rate too rapid to keep fully abreast of everything going on.

Two hours later, Randi had jotted down some practical ideas for Dena and Jordan in producing their own network of archives. Tomorrow she would put together a proposal for them to consider. She glanced at the clock. It was midnight. Time to go to bed. She had work in the morning.

At work the next morning, Randi's mind buzzed with further possibilities for Dena and Jordan.

"Waitress!" A man waved his arm. "I need some more coffee here."

Randi grabbed the brown plastic handle of the glass coffee carafe and headed to the gentleman's table.

A baby at the next table knocked a plate to the floor then started crying. Randi poured the coffee then bent down to clean up the mess.

"I'm so sorry. He never does this at home."

"How old is he?"

"Eleven months." The young mother's smile brightened.

Randi turned to the baby. "Well, you're a cutie." *Even though you toss your plate. What is she thinking, giving a baby his own plate? What's the age when a parent should do that?*

"Miss, where's our order?"

"Should be coming right up. I'll check on it in a moment." Randi finished cleaning up the baby's mess and headed to the kitchen. She blew a strand of hair from her face. "What's up with these people this morning?"

"Order's up," the cook replied. "Just one of those days."

"Ayup," she drawled out in her heaviest Maine accent. Randi washed her hands, dried them off, and went back into the restaurant. She placed the recent order on her tray and headed toward the customer's table.

Lord, I'd really like to be working only one job.

The phone rang. A moment later the cook called out, "Randi, it's for you!"

❧

"Hi, Miranda. I won't keep you, but I wanted you to know I was home. How are you?" Jordan had longed to hear her voice.

"Busy. It's good to hear from you, but I'm afraid I've got to run."

"Okay. What about dinner tonight?"

"Seriously, I don't want to see the inside of another restaurant."

Jordan's heart sank. Maybe she was having second thoughts about their relationship. "All right. Call me when you can."

" 'Bye."

He heard the click of the phone and the electronic hum that followed. He pressed the OFF button and replaced the portable phone in the charger. The bell above the studio door rang. Jordan looked up.

"Hello, Sheriff. How can I help you?"

"Afternoon, Jordan." The sheriff was holding a sheet of white paper. "How was your trip to Niagara?"

"Fine." Did everyone know his comings and goings in this small town?

"Dena said you'd be back sometime this afternoon."

Jordan nodded. The tiny hairs on the back of his neck rose. This wasn't the average customer visit. "What's up?"

"Well, now, that's what I came to talk with you about. Dena said you may have taken this picture at the church fair." He handed Jordan the shot of a girl, with only her face appearing in the picture.

"Yes, sir."

"Have you met her parents?"

"No, sir. I don't believe so."

The sheriff inched his cap further up his head.

"Is there a reason you posted this picture on the Internet?"

"It's a great shot. The girl is adorable. Aside from that, no. Why?"

"Hang on. Let me ask the questions."

"Yes, sir." Jordan's legs started to shake. He'd done nothing wrong, he hoped. So why did he feel as if he was about to be arrested? He looked at the picture again. He couldn't place where or when he'd taken it because the headshot blurred what little there was of the background.

"Jordan, relax. Let me rephrase that. Do you have any other photographs of this child with her parents or of the child speaking with anyone else?"

"No. . .well, I don't know. I can check. I took hundreds of shots that day."

"That would be helpful. This girl looks like a child who was abducted from her home a few months ago."

"Oh, no. Please say it isn't so. She seems so happy."

"Yeah, it is quite a smile. I'd appreciate your going through your pictures from that day."

"No problem. I can pull them up right now."

"Wonderful. Mind if I look over your shoulder?"

"No, not at all."

Jordan pulled up the folder on his computer and loaded the photos from that day. One by one, they clicked through every photograph. Twenty minutes later, they had found no other pictures of the girl. Not even that one. "I'm sorry, Sheriff. I'm not even sure when I took this if it isn't in my computer. It must have been at the church fair. I haven't had an occasion to take other pictures of children playing except then. It's possible the picture was accidentally deleted when I was giving Miranda copies of pictures for my Web page."

The sheriff put his hand on Jordan's shoulder. "No problem. You've done a lot just by taking this picture and posting it on the Internet. The parents are 99 percent certain this is their daughter, but they also received a ransom note a few days after the fair. It had been mailed from the same town the child had been taken in."

"Weird."

"Absolutely. I'm inclined to think the girl is with some family or with someone who was close to the family, in order for her to be so happy. But, then again, I saw a few of my kids in those photographs, and they were having a great time, too. When I'm not on duty I'll come around and order a couple of prints of my kids. But right now, I have to get back with the FBI missing persons unit."

"I understand. I wish I had taken more photographs of her."

"That's all right. No one knew. I'm going to ask around and get folks to check their personal photographs. Does that machine keep track of all the photographs it's printed?"

"Yes, but it's temporary, in case the customer wishes to have another set of prints made. But apart from that, we don't keep those files for long. No more than a week."

"I was afraid of that. Okay—keep your eyes peeled. But don't say anything on the Internet. We don't want to warn the abductors that we're aware they were in the area. With it being a festival, they could have just been traveling through."

Jordan nodded. The way the sheriff's blue eyes focused beyond Jordan, he could tell the officer was already mentally moving on in his investigation.

"Should I remove the picture from my Web page?"

"Let me get back with you on that. I'd like to see what the FBI profiler has to say."

"All right."

"Relax, Jordan. We know you simply took a picture."

Jordan nodded. What could he say? That he was relieved

he wasn't a suspect? At the same time, he was also upset he was even considered a possible suspect. On the other hand, Dena must have put the police at rest about him. Once the sheriff left, Jordan called her. "Hey, Dena. Why didn't you tell me about the girl?"

"Sheriff asked me not to. He wanted to see your reaction. I filled him in on when and how you took that picture."

"Thanks."

"Jordan, I also told the sheriff you were on an assignment at the time of the kidnapping. I'm thankful I had your time-dated photos from your resume to prove where you were then. You're not a suspect, Jordan. The police just needed to be certain."

Jordan let out a pent-up breath.

"You feel crummy, don't you?"

"Absolutely."

"If you need to clear your head, I can come down to the studio for the rest of the day."

"No, I'm fine. It's only a few hours before closing."

"All right. Would you like to come for dinner tonight? I'd love to take another look at your Niagara photos."

Jordan hesitated. Miranda didn't say yes, and she hadn't said no. In fact, she had basically ignored him. "Sure, I'd love to."

"Great. I'll have Wayne bring us some lobsters."

"Count me in for two."

Dena chuckled. "Great. Come on over after you close the studio."

They said their salutations, and Jordan went to work getting caught up on the orders that had come in over the weekend. In the corner of the studio stood his painting of the crab shack. *Maybe I can get back to that soon.*

A couple of customers later, he'd finished sorting the files from the Niagara trip. It had been for a tourism brochure for the state of New York and the Niagara chamber of commerce.

He tapped out a proposal for an article on his trip to Niagara for some travel magazines. If he sold the pictures and the article, he'd have enough to get a new cell-phone service.

He packed the box of negatives he'd brought from his parents' house in the Jeep to make use of Dena's darkroom. It seemed like ages since he had developed a film picture. Even so, several of the shots he'd taken in the Sudan had been printed. Duke sat in the passenger seat on the way to Dena and Wayne's home. Even the natural beauty of the place didn't appeal to him. All he could think about was Miranda and why she was avoiding him again.

fourteen

Randi pushed the button to play her messages as she toed off her shoes. Tonight she would not run. More than likely she wouldn't be running in the morning either. She was sore from head to toe. Every now and again she had one of those days that, no matter what she did, it was never enough for the customers. It was as if all the customers had conspired to take a "nasty" pill before entering the restaurant. In any case, today had been one of those days. A long, hot soak in the tub was top priority.

"Randi," said a voice on the answering machine. "This is Joe from Down-Eastern Solutions. There's a major problem with our Web site. We need you to take care of it ASAP. Call me as soon as you get this message."

Randi glanced up at the clock. She ran to her desk, located the phone number for the company, and placed a call. While she waited for the phone to connect, she pulled up their Web site. What appeared was something totally different, totally inappropriate.

The company's answering machine came on. Randi left a brief message then called Joe's cell phone.

"Randi, it's about time. Where were you?"

"At work. Sorry. What happened?"

"I don't know. We hired a kid to take care of the everyday uploads, and the next thing I know. . ." Joe went on to explain the disaster that was now his Web page. He gave her the contact information for "the kid," and she called him. Fortunately he was only a fifteen-minute drive away and would come over to try to figure out what went wrong.

Then she placed a call to the host servers of the Web site

and verbally worked out a new user name and password. It appeared that someone had sabotaged the Web site. It was rare but did happen from time to time.

Randi glanced at the clock again. She had five minutes to wash her face and freshen up before Michael Robert, aka "the kid," arrived. She whirled through the cottage and pulled a cold piece of pizza from the refrigerator along with a soft drink. No sooner had she taken a bite than Michael Robert knocked on her door.

By two in the morning, Down-Eastern Solutions was up and running, and Randi's day ended in much the same way it had begun. It wasn't until her head hit the pillow that she remembered she hadn't called Jordan back. Nor had she answered his question about going out to dinner that night. Randi's stomach twisted. She tossed and turned until she finally fell fast asleep close to dawn.

ぁ

"Miranda, open up." Her mother was pounding on the door. "Miranda?"

Randi pushed herself off the bed and went to the front door. Her eyes squinted from the bright sunlight.

"Thank the Lord you're all right. I've been trying to reach you for hours. What's the matter? Are you sick?"

"No, I was sleeping."

"Honey, it's three in the afternoon. We were supposed to go out for a late lunch at two today."

"Three?" Randi yawned. "Sorry, Mom. I was up until two this morning fixing a client's Web page."

"Miranda, you have to stop working two jobs. This is killing you."

"I'm fine." She yawned.

"And I'm a monkey's uncle. Go get dressed. I'll make you some coffee."

"Thanks."

Dressing helped wake her up. Randi returned to her mother

and the kitchen a few minutes later.

Her mother chuckled. "You look much better."

"Thanks." Her mother poured the coffee into two cups. Randi joined her at the kitchen table. "I'm sorry about lunch, Mom."

"No problem. You just scared me when you didn't answer your phone."

"I didn't hear it." Randi grabbed the phone and checked for a dial tone. It was there, and she hung it up again. "I didn't fall asleep until dawn."

"Oh, honey, I'm sorry. Do you need to go back to bed?"

"No, I have other work to catch up on."

"All right. Should I go pick up something from the café? I see you haven't had time to shop."

"Sure, that would be nice. A seafood salad for me."

"Okay, I'll be right back."

Randi gave the cottage a clean sweep while her mother went to town and picked up their lunch. She took a few minutes to download her e-mail and was thankful to find no emergencies pending. She also realized she had no messages from Jordan on her answering machine or in her e-mail box.

Jordan. She needed to call him to apologize. She picked up the phone just as her mother walked back in. She replaced it on the charger.

"So tell me about Jordan. What's going on with the two of you?" Her mother put their salads on the table.

Randi sat down after bringing some napkins to the table. "Nothing to tell. We're just friends."

"Right. I wasn't born yesterday. Come on, honey. I've seen the way you look at him."

"Mom, don't you think that until I have something to tell, it should be my own private affair?"

"Maybe, but we live in a small town, and folks are asking me. They saw you leaving his apartment one morning."

Randi's head dropped. "He invited me for breakfast."

"I know, dear. I found that out from Georgette. Heard he made crepes."

"So what is it you want to know?" she asked sharply. "You seem to know it all already."

"Miranda, don't take that tone with me. I'm not trying to be a busybody. I'm concerned. I'm your mother, and I know how hard it has been since you and Cal broke up."

"I'm sorry, Mom. I know you're not trying to tell me how to live my life. And with regard to Jordan, I don't know. We seem to get close; then something happens, and we start fumbling over our words. I'm still nervous, I guess. I want to trust Jordan, but it's hard. Not that he's done anything."

"But Cal breaking your trust has made you leery."

"Exactly." Randi took a forkful of salad and hoped her mother would understand that she didn't want to go too deeply into her feelings for Jordan.

"Jess said Brenda came by for a visit."

"Yeah, that was really hard. You can say you've forgiven someone, but when you're face-to-face with that person, it's hard to believe in giving out grace. Do you know Cal named the baby Tyler? That's the name I picked out when we were dating."

"I can't figure out Cal." Her mother paused with her fork halfway between her mouth and the plate. "If he was so in love with you, why did he cheat on you? And why leave his child like that?"

"Brenda said her in-laws are trying to get custody of Tyler."

"That's sad. I hope they can arrange a visitation plan. Brenda needs to raise her son. But Cal's parents want to see their grandson. Maybe when Mike Collins gets out of the hospital they can work it out."

"Maybe." Randi ate another bite of her salad. "Mom, Jordan wants to be more than friends."

❧

Jordan sat back. The canvas glared at him. Nothing seemed

to be going right since returning from Niagara. Miranda hadn't called, and he'd been rethinking his interest in her. He'd broken one of his rules—not to get involved with a woman until he could take on the responsibility of a wife and children. At his present salary, they'd be eating macaroni and cheese every other night. Miranda deserved better.

"Miserable" described the mood he was in. But time would heal the tear in his heart. He must have misunderstood when he felt God was leading for her to be his wife. How foolish he had been to think he knew the mind of God or God's will for his life.

He glanced back at the canvas. The calm sea had changed to a raging storm on the horizon, just like his own life. A storm hovered around him, nothing really settled. He'd even gone so far as to wonder if he should have taken the job with Dena. How would his life be if he'd stayed in Boston? Would he have landed more contracts with various advertising companies? Dropping his cell service had been an impulsive mistake. No one knew how to reach him. His old roommates had moved out, and that number no longer existed. He was stuck in the boonies with no one to love and tired of feeling sorry for himself.

He tossed the brush in the thinner and left his easel. Walking over to the front bay window, he scanned the area. Duke came up beside him and put his front paws on the window sill. Jordan rubbed the top of the basset hound's head. "Did I make the right decision to move here, boy?"

The summer tourist season was in full swing, and while it doubled the local population, it was a far cry from being a tourist town. Few came to the area with more touristy towns so close by. But there were the exceptions—families who used to live here or whose grandparents lived here. Now they vacationed in the quiet coastal town in the many summer cottages that lined the hills overlooking the harbor.

Sheriff McKean pulled up in front of the store. He marched

toward the door. Jordan reached it before him. "How can I help you, Sheriff McKean?"

"Did you take these?"

Jordan examined the photographs. "Yes."

"Jordan Lamont, you're coming with me."

"What do you need?"

"You don't get it, son, do you?"

"No." Jordan looked back at the photographs. He'd taken them the first or second week he moved to Squabbin Bay, of a child digging for clams while her mother lay on a blanket keeping a watchful eye over her. Jordan examined the picture again. It was the same girl.

"Come on, son. I don't want to arrest you and have to bring you out in cuffs."

"What? You can't possibly believe I had anything to do with that girl's kidnapping."

"Evidence says you're a prime suspect. Not only do you have a picture of the girl, but now you have two. The first was easy for someone to believe you, with so many people at the church festival. But this picture proves you saw Lucy Tomisson before that. The investigators also claim it was a couple, a man and a woman, who kidnapped her. Tell me, where is she? And who is your accomplice?"

"Sheriff McKean, it wasn't me." He wanted to ask how the police found this picture, because he hadn't published it. It was in his personal gallery on his computer. Jordan scanned the studio. His laptop was behind the counter. "Do you mind telling me where you got that picture?"

"Your Web site."

"I didn't—" He bit off his words. If he claimed he hadn't put the picture on his Web site, he might give the impression he had something to hide. "Miranda must have uploaded it."

"Look—I don't care how it got there. But the FBI wants to speak with you ASAP, and they're at my office. You're obviously involved with this case, son, whether innocently or not. I'd like to take your word for it; but you're new here in these parts, and, well, I can't vouch for you."

Jordan swallowed hard. Thoughts of getting a lawyer before being questioned flew through his mind as several television episodes of police shows and movies flickered in instant replay.

"Sheriff McKean, I'll be happy to go there with you, but I have the equipment here to blow up the image."

"They have their own."

"Right. Duke, watch the place. I'll be home soon." Jordan stepped back, grabbed his laptop, and took his first-ever ride in the backseat of a police cruiser. What hit him first was the missing knobs on the rear doors. The bars across the front seat, protecting the officers from criminals, were the second. His heart sank. Fear washed over him. Jordan closed his eyes and prayed. Instantly logic took over. He hadn't been arrested; he was simply being brought in for questioning.

Father, give me peace and the right words to speak. Help me, and help the police find this missing child.

৵

Randi punched in Jess's number on her cell phone. "Jess, it's me. Do you know why the police arrested Jordan?"

"What? When? Are you sure?"

"I just saw him riding in the back of Sheriff McKean's car."

"I don't have a clue. Let me ask Mom. Mom. . ." The word diminished into nothing. Randi figured Jess had covered the phone with her hand.

Moments later, Dena Kearns's voice came through the line. "Randi, it's Dena. What's going on?"

"I don't know. That's why I called Jess. Do you have any idea why the police would arrest Jordan?"

"No, but we can't assume he's been arrested."

"Dena, Sheriff McKean doesn't take people for joyrides in his car." Randi shook her head. She'd done it again—fallen for a man who was not trustworthy. "Dena, I have to go. If you didn't know, I'm glad I could tell you."

Randi used to pride herself on not being judgmental. But today she felt better knowing she hadn't completely fallen in love with Jordan Lamont. Whoever he was, he certainly wasn't the man for her. She had already dealt with one liar in her life, and she didn't need another.

That isn't fair to him, a voice whispered in her head.

Randi paused, looked around to see if someone had spoken then continued walking back to her cottage. She had left her mother convinced she wanted to step out in faith and trust Jordan—only to see him being whisked away in the sheriff's car. *Lord, it isn't fair.*

You're the one not being fair, she argued with herself.

By the time she arrived at the cottage, Jess was sitting in her driveway. "What's going on?" She stood there with her hands on her hips.

"I'm just glad I found out before I was hurt again."

"Randi, you're talking nonsense. You don't know why the police arrested—or if they even arrested—Jordan. You're running scared, and you're not making any sense."

"Drop it, Jess. I can't do this."

Jess relaxed her stance and came up beside Randi. "We need to trust Jordan. He's a good man, Randi."

"I'd like to, but I can't. I just can't."

"Okay, how about a glass of iced tea?"

"Sure."

Jess came inside and didn't say a word while Randi poured two tall glasses of iced tea and sat down at the table.

"Randi, he's not Cal."

"I know, but. . ." *But what?*

"Look, Randi—it's me. I've gone through you and Cal. I know you're afraid, but why don't we wait to see what's going on?"

Randi wrapped her hands around the cool glass of iced tea. It felt good to feel something, anything, to jar her back from the instant betrayal she felt seeing Jordan in the sheriff's car.

Jess reached over and placed a loving hand on her shoulder. "Why don't we pray about this?"

Randi didn't want to explain that she already had. Instead she gave a quick nod of her head and closed her eyes.

"Father, be with Randi right now. Give her the knowledge she needs to trust Jordan or the strength to walk away from him if he's not the man You have designed for her."

Tears edged Randi's eyes.

fifteen

Jordan rubbed his neck as he answered for the fifth time, "No, sir. I do not know these people. I took the picture on April 17th."

"Mr. Lamont, I understand this is frustrating to you, but you do see our problem. You are the only person to have pictures of this child since she was taken from her school," the senior FBI agent said. He pushed back the few remaining hairs from the top of his head.

Why do they do that? Jordan promised himself he would never do that if he started losing his hair. "Yes, sir, but you have the wrong man. If you'd just let me scan through my files, perhaps I have another shot that shows a clearer image of the woman."

"My partner is taking care of that."

Jordan closed his eyes. Something about privacy and needing a warrant popped into his head. On the other hand, Lucy Tomisson's life was at stake. He could put up with a few discomforts. "I can locate the file more easily." He made one last offer.

The agent simply ignored him and looked back at the two blown-up images of the girl. The face of the woman on the beach was hidden by her floppy hat and long hair. *Lord, help us find this little girl.*

"Talk me through your file system." The younger agent, perhaps right out of training, came in holding his laptop.

"I sort my photographs in various ways. Mostly by topic, for easy recovery if someone requests a picture. I also keep a record with a thumbnail sketch of the file as well as a backup of the original file on CDs at home. Search for rev48."

"What does that mean?"

"Revelation chapter four, verse eight. It's where John is writing about the four living creatures in heaven that have eyes all around their heads."

The young agent scrunched his nose. The older man rubbed his hands across those long, thin hairs. Jordan shrugged it off. He'd done that as his own code, a sort of protection if anyone were to try to find his files. Not that anyone would, but "rev48" didn't sound as if it could be that important to the casual looker.

"Got it," the young officer replied. An expletive passed through the man's lips. "What's the password?"

Jordan looked to the senior officer. "Can I type that in privately?"

"Can't you just change it when we're through with it?"

Jordan sighed.

"Jordan," Sheriff McKean said. "Give it up, son."

"You do realize I am aware of all my civil rights being violated here. I have the right to refuse to help. I have the right to call a lawyer. The least you could do is be respectful of my privacy."

"Mr. Lamont, we're not trying to violate your rights. We're simply trying to find a child who has been kidnapped."

"Yes, and you believe I'm a prime suspect. In which case, I have the right to seek legal counsel and to refuse to let you search my computer openly without a warrant."

The young agent slid the computer away from him. "Fine. Call the judge."

"Look—I am simply asking to keep my password a secret—" Jordan stopped himself. "Fine. The password is 'rjjakm79.'"

"What does that stand for?" Sheriff McKean asked. "I'm not familiar with that biblical book."

"It stands for Roger, June, Jordan, Adam, Katie, and Michael, and seventy-nine is the year my parents got married."

"Ah."

"I'm in." The young agent rubbed his hands together. His eyes sparkled. *He truly believes I'm guilty, Lord.*

"Now go to April of this year. You'll see a listing of all the pictures I took according to the series. If you read them off, I'll be able to tell you which set that picture came from."

"Flowers, trees, birds, shore, mountains, family at play—"

"That's it."

"It's not linked to the photos." The agent's shoulders slumped.

Jordan closed his eyes and prayed for the Lord's grace one more time. "No, they are not linked. I simply keep an accounting in this file of what series I took that month. Now find 'fapme.'"

"What is this, Fort Knox?"

"No, but it is my livelihood. Open the folder 'fapme' and select to read the group as a list."

"There're about two hundred photos here."

"I honestly can't tell you from here which photos to look at. But you can select them all and hit the open apple key and the letter *O* key, and it will open all of them so you can simply click through them."

"You'd think with you being a professional photographer you'd use the better software."

Jordan resisted the cutting remark he wanted to say and simply replied, "It's on there. I don't upload all the raw files to it."

"Oh," the younger agent mumbled.

"Now, while Agent Wilkes is looking, would you mind going over the details one more time with me?" the older agent asked.

Yes! he wanted to scream in frustration. Jordan turned toward the sheriff, who was putting his hat back on his head. "I need to go out on patrol."

"I want you here!" Jordan demanded. "I'm here of my own

free will, but I need a witness, just in case."

The sheriff removed his hat and sat down again. "All right."

"Now as I was asking. . ."

⁊⁊

Randi fought with herself all day knowing she should give Jordan a chance to explain what happened. But why go through that kind of misery? Would she ever be able to trust someone again? Had Cal robbed her of being able to trust people? No, she still trusted many people. But men, especially single men, or rather men she wanted to date, were the problem. Jordan was the only man she wanted to date.

Randi huffed as she lay down on her bed for the night. Jordan hadn't called. Not that she expected him to. But then again she did. She wondered if he was still down at the police station and fought the desire to check after Jess went home.

She wanted to trust him. She prayed he was the man she thought him to be. But then she had prayed for Cal, too. And what did she and Jordan really have in common with one another? She loved to run; he hated to exercise. He spent hours in the mud just for a picture. She wouldn't be caught dead playing in the muck of low tide.

She woke to the same thoughts the next morning. After a hearty run, she went past the studio and saw no evidence of Jordan being awake. Back at home, she readied herself for work. Just as she was about to leave, her phone rang.

"Hello."

"Hey, Randi. It's Cal."

"Cal?"

"Yeah, look—I'm in the neighborhood, and I wanted to speak with you."

Randi thought it odd that Cal would be in the area a couple of days after Brenda moved down to Portland. Obviously his parents or someone was keeping him well informed. "What do you want to talk about?"

He hemmed and hawed. "I'd prefer to speak in person."

"Cal, I don't have anything to say. And if you're thinking I might be interested in getting back together with you, you're sadly mistaken."

"No, no, it's nothing like that. I heard Brenda spoke with you before she left town."

Randi rolled her shoulders to work out the building stress. "I have nothing to say about that."

"Come on, Rand. It's me. I need your help here."

Her mind flew back to the issue of his parents trying to get custody of the baby. "No, Cal. I'm not getting involved."

"But, Rand, I'm not allowed to see my own kid."

"Maybe you should have thought about that before you ran off and left Brenda and the baby alone. Cal, for once in your life, be a man. Support your child and do the right thing by Brenda. Stop fooling around and take responsibility for your own actions."

An expletive flew through the phone lines. "I knew I couldn't count on you—a woman scorned and all that."

"Cal, stop it. This has nothing to do with you and me; this has to do with you and how you treat people. You're a spoiled kid who's never grown up. Try growing up and being a man." She hung up the phone and ran out the door and headed for the car. She knew his pattern. He would call again. He would continue to badger her until she did what he wanted her to do.

Getting behind the wheel, she turned the ignition and drove off to nowhere in particular, ruminating over how her personal life couldn't get more miserable. She prayed Cal would not continue his normal pattern and move on.

She thought about calling her mother and telling her about Cal's call. She thought about calling Jess. Instead she called Jordan. On the fourth ring, the answering machine picked up. Randi snapped her phone shut. Could she really trust him anyway? Out of the corner of her eye, she spotted Jordan's vehicle at the police station.

Randi's entire body shook. She tightened her grasp on the steering wheel and headed out of town. Why couldn't life be simpler?

૨*

Four hours later, the lunch rush was in full swing at the restaurant. Randi's feet ached. Her mind buzzed about Jordan, Cal, and Brenda. She knew without asking Cal that he wanted Randi to give him some kind of information that would allow him to get custody of the baby. Or rather for his parents to get custody. No judge in his right mind would give custody to a father who had deserted his wife and child, would he? No. Any parent who could do that once could do it again. At least she hoped such logic would prevail in the courts and not Cal's parents' way of paying for what they wanted.

Randi said another prayer for Brenda and the baby. Brenda was changing. Cal showed no signs of change.

The bell over the restaurant door rang. Jordan stood there with two men dressed in black business suits. All she could think of was the movie *Men in Black*. "Miranda." Jordan came up to the counter. "Honey, it's good to see you."

"Who are your friends?"

"They're with the FBI. They'd like to talk with you."

Me? She wanted to scream.

"They have some questions for you."

"Miss Miranda Blake?"

"Yes." She nodded and balled up the dishcloth she held in her hand.

"Please advise your superiors that we need to speak with you."

Randi stepped back to the kitchen. "Jake, there're some men—"

"We know." Jake slapped the spatula on the grill. "Send them in to me."

"Okay."

Randi went back to the FBI agents. What could Jordan

have done to get the FBI involved? "My manager wants to speak with you. He says to go back there."

The counter bell rang. "Randi, pick up for table four."

"Excuse me."

❧

Jordan couldn't believe Miranda's manager had convinced the agents to sit down for lunch and wait until the rush was over. They ordered Reuben sandwiches and ate without saying a word to one another. Jordan also couldn't believe they still didn't trust him. *Once they sit down with Miranda, I hope they'll see I've been telling the truth.*

Miranda came to the table. She looked worn-out and suspicious. She must have heard they'd taken him to the police station yesterday. Squabbin Bay was a small town, and news traveled quickly. Unfortunately the truth about why he'd been brought in would not spread. Only rumors. He'd been ordered not to talk about it.

"Mr. Lamont, would you please excuse us?" Agent O'Malley rubbed the crumbs off his white shirt.

"Sure." Jordan stood.

"Don't go too far," Agent Wilkes added.

Jordan nodded and left the restaurant. He'd wait outside for them. The piercing look he'd received from Miranda when he left gave him a good idea what she was probably thinking.

He couldn't blame her, with what had happened between her and Cal. *On the other hand, doesn't she know me well enough to know I'm not like that?*

Jordan leaned against the black sedan. They hadn't even allowed him to drive his own vehicle. He scanned the area looking for a telephone booth. He spotted a phone on the corner of a building a half block away. He wanted to talk with Dena. The sheriff had promised him he would call her, but she should hear everything from him.

He reached into his pocket and pulled out two quarters

then tapped out Dena's number. On hearing her answering machine, he left a detailed message of the events over the past couple of days. Jordan still hadn't been arrested, but he wasn't free to leave either. He was heading back to the restaurant when he noticed an art supply store down the street. He could use some more oils for his painting. He rounded the corner in time to be tackled to the ground.

Wilkes whispered in his ear, "I told you not to run off."

Jordan groaned. "I was going to the art supply store."

"Yeah, right. I know you're involved here. I just can't prove it. Yet. You're not going anywhere—got that?"

Jordan had had enough. "I want a lawyer. Now. I've had enough. I've cooperated with you all the way. I've given you more information than you had. And yet you still suspect me. I want a lawyer now. I know my rights."

Agent Wilkes pulled him up from the ground. "You gave up your rights when—"

Agent O'Malley had followed Wilkes out and gave the younger agent a stern look of reproof.

"I did not kidnap her," Jordan repeated.

"We'll see." Wilkes slapped handcuffs on his wrists and started back to the restaurant.

"What are you doing, Wilkes?" Agent O'Malley demanded.

"He was running away."

"I doubt it. Take off those cuffs."

"But, sir."

"Wilkes!" Agent O'Malley bellowed.

Agent Wilkes removed the cuffs. "I'll get you yet," Wilkes whispered. Then he added in full voice, "He lawyered up."

"I would have done it yesterday. Let's get back to Squabbin Bay."

He could see Miranda standing near the window, her eyes filled with tears. She turned and ran toward the back.

"May I make a call?" Jordan asked.

"Sure," Agent O'Malley said. "We'll wait for you in the car."

Jordan went to the payphone by the door in the restaurant and dialed his parents. "Dad, I can't explain right now, but I need a criminal lawyer ASAP."

Jordan scanned the room for Miranda. "No, Dad, I'm fine. I'll explain later. Just contact who you can and have them send a lawyer to the Squabbin Bay police station."

"Are you sure you're all right?"

"Yes. It's a misunderstanding. But one man is convinced I'm guilty. I really can't talk right now, Dad. Please call one of your lawyers and have them connect with someone in my area."

"All right, son. You be careful, okay?"

"I will. I'll be fine. But please pray for the situation. An innocent life could be in danger."

"Son, I wish you hadn't said that. Now I'll be fretting all afternoon until you can explain."

"I will as soon as I'm able. But I'm all right. I'm just tired of the nonsense from this one agent."

"Agent?"

"Please, Dad, no more questions. I have to go."

"Oh, all right. I'll get Larry right on it."

"Thanks."

Miranda stepped from the back kitchen with a tray of entrées.

"Miranda—"

"Stay away, Jordan."

"What?"

"Just stay away. I can't handle this right now."

Jordan lifted his hands in surrender. Deep in his heart he'd known she would respond this way. He had to trust that the Lord would work things out. Unfortunately God's timing was always slower than his own, or so it seemed.

sixteen

Wild thoughts ran through Randi's mind. Why would the FBI want to question her for putting a picture on Jordan's Web site without his knowledge? Why didn't they believe him? She'd found the picture of a child playing on the beach with the mother watching in his files of photographs and uploaded it. It was a touching picture. She'd even taken just the face of the child and blown it up to a full-size print. But the agents said the little girl had been taken from her parents. They obviously suspected Jordan of being a part of the kidnapping, which didn't make sense.

When she got home, she searched the Internet. After hours of hunting, she found a Web site with a picture of the girl Jordan had photographed then followed up on that information and found news releases about Lucy Tomisson's abduction. Randi's stomach twisted just thinking about it. Why would anyone steal a child?

One thing was clear—it was not an act Jordan would have participated in. No matter what Agent Wilkes said. Jordan wasn't that kind of man—which made her wonder if she should be questioning his actions, either. "Father, bring clarity to this situation."

She reached for the phone to call Jordan then pulled her hand back. As much as she wanted to talk with him, she was still unsure if it was the wisest move to make. And why hadn't he called her? Shouldn't he be home by now? Glancing at the clock, she decided it was too late to call anyway.

Instead of going to bed, she worked for a few hours on some of her clients' Web pages. By midnight, she finally went to bed and fell into fitful slumber. The battle of trusting

Jordan waged on in her dreams for a second night.

The next morning, she woke tired and sore. Today she would run the full five miles before getting ready for work. Yesterday she'd run only three. She needed the release of endorphins in her brain to kill off the pain. She finished her five miles, showered, dressed, and ran out the door to go to work when she saw Cal sitting against the hood of her car.

"Cal?"

"Hey, Randi."

She walked to her car door. "Excuse me, but I have to go to work."

"Rand, I really need your help."

You really need the Lord's. "I can't help you, Cal."

"Don't you understand? I won't be allowed to see my son."

Then you should have thought about that before you left your wife. "I can't help you, Cal. Speak with Brenda. She's your wife."

"That's the problem, isn't it? You won't help me because I wouldn't marry you."

Anger rode up her spine. "To be honest, that is not why. Your problems with Brenda are your problems, not mine. I don't want to and won't have anything to do with you."

"I don't get it. All those thoughts and plans we put together for years. How can they die just like that?"

"Cal, you have a problem. First of all, you couldn't be faithful to me in our dating relationship."

"I—"

She held up her hand to stop him then continued. "Second, you're forgetting you're married to the mother of your child. What have you done to try to make that relationship right? How can you fix your marriage? I'm not interested in marrying you and haven't been for a long time. You and I were a mistake. I just assumed we'd naturally get married when we were older. But that wasn't meant to be."

"But, Randi, I still love you."

"You don't love me. You love yourself. Put your wife and child first. Try that and see if your life changes."

"I am thinking of my child first. If he comes and lives with me, I'll see him almost every day."

"Almost? Just listen to yourself. You aren't thinking straight. Who's more important, you or the child?"

Cal opened his mouth then stopped.

"I know you were going to say you then thought I wanted to hear 'the child.' You don't get it. Why don't you go talk with Pastor Russell? Maybe he can help you understand."

"I don't need God."

"Oh, yes, you do. Look how wonderful your life has turned out without Him. You're a man who would run out on his family. You'd leave your wife and child hungry rather than be responsible for them."

"I knew there was a reason we never got married."

"Exactly. We weren't meant to."

"No, it's because you think you're so special and holy. Why don't you get off your cloud and come live with the rest of us?"

And to think he came to me for help. Give me grace, Lord. "You're right. I am special. I'm a child of God, and He loves me so much that He died for me. He lives inside me and helps me deal with"—she didn't want to be spiteful—"deal with situations in my life that aren't always pleasant."

"Randi, look. I didn't come to argue with you. I simply wanted you to testify that I'm a better parent for Tyler than Brenda."

Randi chuckled. "I'm sorry, Cal, but I can't do that. In my book, you aren't." She opened the car door and slipped inside before Cal could respond then rolled down the window. "Don't get a court order, because I will not help your case."

Cal stepped away from her car. *Lord, please get through to him. He needs You. He needs to grow up.*

She turned the key and started the engine. Putting the car in reverse, she backed down the driveway and onto the street then shifted into drive and headed toward work. She saw Mabel pushing her shopping cart out to her car and waved. The older lady smiled and waved back.

Randi clicked on her cell phone and auto-dialed Jordan's number. On hearing the answering machine, she hung up and continued on to work. *He couldn't possibly be at the police station still, could he?*

❧

Jordan couldn't thank his father enough for the quick response of finding him an attorney. To say the attorney was happy with how cooperative Jordan had been with the authorities was an overstatement. Legally, Jordan should not have given them so much freedom. Morally, he felt as if he had no choice. But with Agent Wilkes out to prove him responsible, an attorney was necessary to protect him. They spent a little over an hour reviewing the past two days; then the attorney excused himself, and five minutes later Jordan was walking out of the police station.

"Thank you." Jordan extended his hand.

"My pleasure. Remember—if they call you in again, you call me. My office is in Ellsworth. But I've informed them that if they need to speak with you again, they are to contact me and I'll get in touch with you. Don't say another word. I understand your wanting to help them find the little girl. But Wilkes is convinced you're guilty. Be very careful."

"I will." Jordan put his hand in his pocket to retrieve his keys and touched the business card the lawyer had given him. He hoped he would not have to use it.

He returned to the studio and went to work. Dena had everything in order, and tomorrow there would be an early morning studio appointment for a family portrait. He glanced down at the number. Ten people. He hoped they were older and able to listen to instructions; patience would be in short supply after the grueling time with Agent Wilkes.

It felt good to be working. Dena had covered for him,

but he wanted to keep working for her. He prayed she still trusted him.

The next day the family arrived, and the session went very well. Dena came in and went over some of the bookwork while he finished up with the family. After the last person left, she spoke up. "You were good with them."

"Thanks. I was concerned the weariness of the past few days would get the better of me. I'm just grateful the baby was sleeping most of the time."

Dena chuckled. "I hear you. So what's happened with the police investigation?"

"If they would leave me alone and try to find Lucy, it might help."

Dena's eyes widened. "They think—"

"Not all of them—just one," he interrupted. "He thinks I must have been a part of everything and that my pictures were going to be used somehow for the ransom."

"Oh, no. Why would he think that?"

"Because I unwittingly took another photograph of Lucy Tomisson."

"What? When?"

"About the second week I was here. I was just out taking photos when I came across this mother and child at the beach. The girl was in her glory. The mother seemed happy, but something in her eyes seemed more distant. Looking back, I'd say she was thinking about what she'd done or how much time they'd be spending with the child. Unfortunately the photo does not capture the woman's face. I can't wait until the police find Lucy alive and leave me out of it."

Dena settled into a chair. "Wayne and I were going on a shoot next week in Florida. Do you want me to find someone else to cover it?"

"May I?" He smiled. The getaway would be nice. "Joking. I know the sheriff wants me in the area."

"Would you like Wayne to speak with the sheriff? They

go a long way back."

"No, I'm fine. I called my dad and had an attorney sent to the station after the second day of Agent Wilkes's not bothering to look at any information, except to twist things so it looked like I was guilty. I gave them two days of my time without a lawyer to try to help. After that, I'd had enough."

"I doubt I would have given them more than an hour." Dena stood up and patted him on the back. "Hang in there, Jordan. The Lord will get you through."

Jordan respected Dena's faith and appreciated her confidence in him that he wasn't a suspect in her eyes. He wished he could say the same for Miranda. Her suspicious, dark gray eyes from yesterday still haunted him. "He's what I'm trusting in. If you wouldn't mind, I'd like to go over to the point where I took those pictures. It would be nice if the lady and child were there again."

"Do you think it wise to go? Wayne and I have been on a stakeout before. Maybe we could lend a hand, as well."

"You know, if we could set up a team to stake out the area—"

The phone rang.

"Hello," Dena answered. A moment later her face paled, but she said nothing. She motioned for a pen. Jordan reached for one and handed it to her. She wrote something down then handed it to Jordan.

He read the note. *FBI is listening.* His temper rose another notch; then he told himself to settle down. Agent Wilkes believed him guilty. The man had to follow his leads. Unfortunately it wasn't helping that little girl. He hoped Wilkes would move on and look for Lucy Tomisson's real abductors.

"Sure, Sally, we can work that out. Tell Brad he can come to my place this evening. Wayne would love to see him." Dena paused and gave Jordan a thumbs-up.

Something was going on with this phone call. Who was Sally, and how would she know the FBI was listening in on their conversation?

"Great. See you tonight." Dena hung up the phone. "Jordan, on second thought, we probably should leave it to the authorities to investigate." She scribbled down another message. *Play along with what I say.*

"You're probably right. I just wish I could do something for that little girl." Jordan read the next note. *Tonight—my house with Sheriff McKean.* Jordan nodded his agreement.

"I know. But we can pray."

"I've been doing that since the first visit from the sheriff." He wanted to say so much more but figured he shouldn't.

"Well, I've done my bookwork. I need to get ready for Brad and Sally coming over tonight. Wayne and I will go to Florida as we've planned. I'm sure things will work out here."

"I know they will. I'm innocent."

"I know, and eventually Agent Wilkes will know, as well." She smiled.

Jordan held back a chuckle. He could have so much fun knowing Agent Wilkes was listening. But then again, that would let Wilkes know he was exposed.

"I'll call you later."

"Sure."

"Do we have any scheduled appointments for the rest of the day?"

"Nope."

"Good. Why don't you finish that painting today and take your mind off things?"

She pointed to the photograph on his computer of the abducted little girl.

"You know, that doesn't sound like a bad idea. I could use the relaxation."

Dena left after a brief hug and slipped her cell phone into his hand. Cell phones were one of the easiest devices to listen in on. He slid it into his pocket. He understood he was to meet the sheriff at her house tonight, but only after he spent the rest of the day out at the point, painting, waiting, praying that Lucy would show up. He grabbed his portable easel and paints and headed out the door. He loaded the Jeep, forcing himself not to look at the street. "Come on, Duke."

❧

"Randi, it's Jess," Randi heard on her cell phone.

"Hey, Jess. What's up?"

"First, I'm wondering how you are after the other night."

"I'm fine."

"Yeah, right, and you're ready to run the marathon this week."

Randi chuckled. "Okay. I'm okay. I'm trying to look at Jordan in a better light. I had a visit from Cal this morning."

"Cal? What does that cad want?"

"He wants me to testify that he'd be a better parent for his child than Brenda."

"No way."

Randi checked the rearview mirror then glanced at the road ahead of her. "That's basically what I said to him, as well."

"I want to hear all the details, but I can't talk long. You need to come to my house tonight. Something major is going on, and Jordan needs our help. Well, actually a little girl needs our help."

"Wait. What are you talking about?"

"You know Jordan was speaking with the sheriff, right?"

"Yeah, and they came to see me at the restaurant, as well."

"Oh, man. Look—one of the FBI agents is out to get Jordan. The sheriff doesn't buy it, and he wants to find this little girl ASAP. For her sake as well as to clear Jordan of any wrongdoing."

Randi's heart went out to him.

"Anyway, they're listening to Jordan at his place."

"They bugged the studio?"

"Not exactly. They have one of those listening devices where they can sit in the car and aim it at the area they want to listen to. It looks kinda like a gun with a minisatellite dish on it. The whole town is in a buzz over it. Jordan's out at the point painting. We're hoping they're going to stop watching him after a few hours and start looking for the girl. Mom gave him her cell phone. She's going to call him later on this evening and ask him to bring the phone by our place. The FBI can't listen at our house unless they come closer in on the driveway. Sheriff McKean is coordinating this. Anyway, come to my place tonight."

"I'll be there."

"Great."

Randi wanted to ask more questions but kept it to one. "Is this all my fault?"

"Huh?"

"I put those pictures on his Web site. I thought it was a beautiful picture of a family's emotional bond."

"Randi, this isn't your fault. Maybe it's God's way of helping this little girl. You and Jordan didn't know she'd been abducted. This could be what saves her and returns her to her family."

Randi's eyes filled with tears. She pulled into a store parking lot to get a grip on her own emotions. "Can I call him on your mom's cell?"

"No, they can listen in on a cell-phone call."

Randi's stomach flipped. How could they believe Jordan guilty? How could she?

seventeen

Jordan sensed that the car driving back and forth on the road behind him was probably Agent Wilkes. He forced himself to concentrate on the bluff in the foreground of the painting. He wanted to go to the beach where he'd taken the picture of the child but knew that if he did, the FBI would take him in for questioning again. So he settled on an area one would drive past to get to that beach. Dena's phone weighed heavily in his pocket. He wasn't sure why he had it but knew it involved something about the meeting with the sheriff tonight at Dena's house.

Jordan put down his brush and set it in the jar with thinner. He wiped his hands and grabbed his camera. He clicked off a couple of shots from where he was painting then walked over to the water's edge and concentrated on the various tidal pools formed from the outgoing tide. Inside them, he found baby shrimp, horseshoe crabs, and minnows. He had no reason to photograph these pools, but it seemed easier to get lost in photography than in painting at the moment. He knelt down and switched his digital to macro settings and worked his way down the beach. Each pool had its own unique characteristics. Two-thirds of the walls around the pool in front of him now were granite rock. The last third was thick, coarse, brown sand. Inside the pool, a row of snails lined a crack in the rock. At the other end of the granite edge, a colony of baby mussels held on to the rock's edge with their brown, stringy beards. A small starfish wrapped itself around an even smaller baby clam. Just then a baby eel popped out and attempted to take the clam away from the starfish. Jordan clicked off some rapid pictures, hoping to catch the eel in action.

He watched closer as the barnacle on the rock face opened to catch the plankton that was also trapped in the pool. It always amazed him how creative God was when He crafted the various life forms on this earth. Not that he had a heart for barnacles, since they could tear the bottom of a person's foot when walked on—not to mention the infection that could set in if the wound wasn't cleaned well. But they served a purpose somehow. He didn't know what that purpose could be, though, since barnacles were the bane of most boat owners. Jordan smiled and snapped a few more pictures. Then he added some different filters to see the difference they would make on the tidal-pool shots.

Eventually Duke got tired of waiting for him and came moseying down the shoreline, disturbing the tidal pools. Jordan chuckled and took some pictures of his four-legged buddy. He found a small piece of driftwood. "Fetch, Duke."

Duke lifted his head and watched as the stick landed in the water. Slowly he ambled over to it and picked it up. Basset hounds weren't known for their speed, and the years had taken their toll on Duke. He still loved to fetch, but one or two tosses were all the old boy could handle.

"Atta boy, Duke." Jordan gave the dog a hearty rubdown. "At least you still love me."

Duke slobbered kisses over Jordan. "All right, boy. That's enough."

An hour passed before he knew it. Relaxed, he and Duke walked back to his easel. Jordan knew he was boring Agent Wilkes, but there seemed to be some poetic justice involved. Jordan's smile broadened as he dipped his brush in a blend of color that resembled the rock in the shadow of the bluff.

His mind drifted to Miranda. She was like that rock, hidden in the shadow of her past relationship with Cal. *Lord, help her move on and trust me, please.*

He hadn't sensed Agent Wilkes for quite a while. He turned toward the road and glanced up and down. Not seeing anything, he returned to his painting.

A short time later, Dena's cell phone rang. He checked the display and saw the word *Home*. "Hello?"

"Hey, Jordan, did you find my cell phone?"

"Yeah, I was going to drop it off later this evening. Need it sooner?"

"Nope. Later is fine."

"I'll bring it over as the sun starts to go down."

"That will be great. Can I add you to our supper list?"

"Do you have enough? Can I bring anything? You know I won't turn down a home-cooked meal."

Dena chuckled. "Nah, Wayne will fire up the grill, and I have everything else under control."

"Thanks for the invite. I'll see you later."

"Great. Bye." Dena hung up the phone.

Jordan hoped Agent Wilkes would get the message. He'd been tempted to use the phone and call Miranda, but it wasn't his, and he still hadn't ordered a new service yet. He really needed to do that.

Plus, he wasn't sure she wanted to talk with him yet. The haunted look in her eyes still caused a shiver to run up and down his spine. *Lord, please help her.*

❧

Randi wiped the tears from her eyes and drove the rest of the way home. She passed Jordan's driveway only to see his vehicle wasn't there. At home, she opened her computer files to the job she was contracted to do for Jess and the lobstermen co-op she had put together.

Dena had supplied some great photographs to go on the Web site. Randi tweaked the header of the Web page to be a collage of various shots of the lobster industry with a huge, five-pound, steamed lobster on a platter in the center. It made Randi's stomach rumble just seeing it.

Remembering she'd been too upset to eat much for a few days, she raided the fridge. As she grabbed a lobster roll her mother had left the day before, she remembered the picture she'd put on Jordan's Web site. The FBI had removed it, but she had her own copy. She opened the picture on the computer and stared at it. She knew exactly which beach Jordan had photographed. Grabbing the sandwich and keys, she headed for the point. As she approached the bend in the road out to the point, she noticed a dark sedan parked on the side of the road. Around the bend, she found Jordan's Jeep and him sitting at his easel. She pulled over. "Jordan!" she called.

He turned and jumped up from his easel.

"Miranda, what are you doing here?"

"I know where you took that picture. I put it on the Internet. It's the same picture, Jordan. I blew it up for the facial shot. I'm—"

Jordan held his finger to her lips. A shiver of joy spread through her. He leaned in closer and whispered, "I don't know if I'm being watched."

The dark sedan popped into her mind. "There's a car around the bend."

"Ah, I'm not surprised. I was hoping Wilkes would be bored by now."

"I think he's asleep."

Jordan laughed. "Come." He held her by the hand and led her down to the beach. When they were down at the water's edge, he brushed her hair away from her face and gazed into her eyes. "I do love your eyes."

Miranda blinked. His own hazel ones captivated her attention. She raised her hand and pulled the elastic band from his hair and wove her fingers through the long, wavy strands. "Do you know how much I've wanted to do that ever since I've met you?"

Jordan held her tighter. "I love you. I'm sorry about what is happening. But, trust me, I've done nothing wrong."

"I know," she whispered. "I'm sorry for not trusting you."

Jordan squeezed her. She felt his protective love encircling her. "I've never been so afraid of losing anyone's respect as I have been about losing yours."

"I'm sorry."

"I had a visit from Cal this morning."

He pulled back and held on to her shoulders. "What happened?"

"He wanted me to testify that he would be a better parent than Brenda."

"You've got to be kidding. Does this guy have no clue? He ran off on his wife and child. What is he thinking?"

"He isn't. He's always had what he wanted. He smooth-talked me for years. Maybe losing his son will help him grow up. I don't know. But what really bothered me was that he thought I would let him back in my life."

She felt Jordan stiffen.

"Relax. It's okay. I handled it. He knows I'm not interested in being involved with him."

Jordan caressed her cheek. She leaned into his fingers. She'd never felt so close to Cal as she did to Jordan. She closed her eyes, and her voice caught. "Jordan, I love you."

Jordan scooped her in his arms. "Miranda, you don't know how long I've waited to hear that. Woo-hoo!" he hollered and spun her around.

Duke howled in unison.

She held on as joy flooded her senses. A peace, a connection with Jordan, cemented within her. He was the one her soul longed to unite with. All the fears and doubts from the past melted away. She kissed his cheek. He stood perfectly still and eased her back down onto her feet. "Kiss me," she whispered.

"With pleasure." Their lips met, and a deeper sense of connection and oneness fused within her. Her pulse raced. Slowly she pulled away and rested her head on his chest.

Neither of them spoke. They stood there for a moment,

caught in the intimacy of the moment. Then she pulled back and looked into his eyes. "I love you."

"I love you, too."

Jordan stiffened.

"What's the matter?"

"Agent Wilkes is standing behind a tree."

She'd forgotten he'd been out there following Jordan. Watching. A wave of nausea swept over her at the mere thought. Randi swallowed. "Should I go? I'll be at Jess's tonight."

Jordan stepped back. "I'll see you later."

&

Jordan opened and closed his fist several times as he watched Agent Wilkes stare at Miranda while she walked to her car. He followed at least ten paces behind then went to his easel. He had no desire to paint, not now, not when he should be with Miranda. But he had little choice. The only thing he was happy about was that the agent wasn't holding his listening device and could not have heard the conversation between them.

He sat down at the easel and picked up a brush. Dipping it in the burnt sienna and mixing it with a touch of green, he placed the brush next to the bush he was painting in the foreground. He'd never sell this painting. The best he could hope for was to scrape off what he had done and paint over the canvas. There was nothing of interest in the painting. And if he couldn't find anything in the picture, a customer sure wouldn't.

He decided to change the picture to a surreal painting instead of the more traditional impressionist one. It fit his mood better. Moments later, a surrealist image of Wilkes's head, protruding out of the stone bluff, developed on his canvas. Jordan laughed and continued with the wild rendition.

An hour later, he finished the painting. Picking up his gear, he loaded his Jeep and walked over to the agent's car with the canvas in hand. "Here ya go, Wilkes. Enjoy!"

"Hey, what—? I don't look like that."

"Perhaps not, but it sure felt good painting you that way. Have a good night."

Wilkes pulled out of his parking place before Jordan reached the door. By the time Jordan drove back to town, he expected the agent to be stationed outside his apartment. As he drove past the sheriff's office, he noticed Wilkes's car and the sheriff's parked outside.

Instead of going home, he headed back out of town for Dena and Wayne's. Dena's red convertible Mercedes was parked out front alongside Wayne's four-wheel-drive pickup.

"Jordan," Dena greeted him at the door. "Come in. You're early."

"Agent Wilkes is at the sheriff's station. . . ." His words trailed off. Sheriff McKean sat on the living room sofa. "Sheriff."

"Relax, son. Remember, I called this meeting."

"What about Wilkes?"

"He's doing some busywork at my office. I had my secretary draw up a list of recent home purchases in the area."

Jordan sat down on the rattan chair in the corner of the room.

"Jordan, can I get you anything?" Dena asked. "Soda? Iced tea?"

"Iced tea will be fine."

"Good. Wayne has the steaks marinating, so we should be eating in an hour," she said and headed into the kitchen. "A few more will be coming in a half hour."

He wanted to ask who and why but simply nodded.

"Jordan," the sheriff said. "First off, I don't believe you're guilty. And I do believe you had a wonderful idea in staking out the point. But with Wilkes convinced you're part of the child's abduction, I think it best if we organize and stake out the point in shifts. After all, if that little girl is in my territory, I want to find her. I certainly don't want to spend days talking to the same person over and over again."

Jordan sat back and smiled. "Thanks for the vote of confidence."

"I'm glad you called the attorney. If you hadn't, I was going to do it for you. Enough is enough."

"I don't mean to be telling you your job, sheriff, but aren't you breaking some laws by informing me I was being listened to?"

"Nope. He didn't get a court order, which means he's disobeying the law. I pointed that out to him when I radioed him to come in from his surveillance."

Interesting. "If Agent Wilkes feels he's above the law, I'll need to be careful he doesn't fabricate my involvement."

"I don't believe he'll do that. But I do want to be careful you are with someone at all times."

After a knock at the door, a half-dozen people came in. Most Jordan didn't recognize. Among them were Sally, the sheriff's secretary; and her husband, Doug. Jim Baxter he'd seen a time or two in church. And a Bob and Marie from someplace. Jordan didn't catch their last name or their connection. He shook hands and sat down.

After thirty minutes, the house was full. It was established that six teams of two would go out on four-hour stretches. Miranda walked in the door as Wayne finished cooking the steaks on the grill. In the end, Jordan learned that most of the people were volunteers for Squabbin Bay's fire department and other emergency services.

Miranda sat down beside him at the picnic table and slipped her hand into his. "Hi." She kissed him on the cheek.

"Hi. I'm really sorry Wilkes busted in on us."

The lilt of her laughter caused his heart to skip a beat. "Do you think he has a tape?"

"What?"

"Might be fun to listen to it several years from now."

Jordan roared with laughter. Everyone turned and faced them. Miranda buried her face in his chest. "Sorry."

By the end of the night, Jordan felt so welcomed and a part of this community that he never wanted to go back to the city. He understood completely why Dena had moved up here. And with God's blessings, he and Miranda would have the same joyful reasons in the future.

The sheriff's radiophone rang. "Sheriff McKean, Agent O'Malley here. We have a lead. Can you come in?"

eighteen

Randi snuggled up beside Jordan as the sheriff took the call.

"I'll be right there." Sheriff McKean turned toward the group anxiously awaiting further information. "Nothing to tell, folks. But you'll need to take care of one last order of business in my absence. Who's spending the night with Jordan?"

The sheriff left without another word.

"I have the dead-man's shift at the firehouse tonight. Sorry. I can do it tomorrow though," Jim Baxter offered.

"I can do it," Steve Healy called out. "Do you snore?"

Jordan chuckled. "Not that I'm aware of."

Randi wondered and hoped she would find out one day. The thought caught her up short. She'd just kissed Jordan, and now she was thinking marriage. *Get a grip, girl.*

Wayne Kearns smiled. "Let's take this one day at a time. Let's stop and have a word of prayer for this little girl."

Everyone joined hands, and Wayne led them in a brief but touching prayer. As folks started to leave, they made their way to Jordan and gave him their individual support. Randi couldn't have been more proud of her hometown.

Jess pulled her aside and out to the deck. "So what's going on with the two of you?"

"Nothing."

"Girl, this is me you're talking to. Give."

"We made up this afternoon."

"I'd say made up. You believe him, don't you?" Jess sat on the rail of the deck, smiling. She seemed so content.

Randi prayed Jess would find what she'd found in Jordan. "Jess, I love him."

"That was pretty obvious. So come on—details."

"Ask Agent Wilkes. He might just have it on tape."

"No." Jess jumped back to her feet. "For real? Video or audio?"

"Audio, I think." A smile spread across her face to think that Agent Wilkes might have a video of her and Jordan's first kiss.

Jess laughed. "You kissed him, didn't you?"

"I'll never tell."

Jess's laughter increased. "You don't have to. And to think the first time you met the man you dumped two bowls of lobster bisque on him."

Randi giggled. "Don't remind me." She paused. "Might be fun to have it at the wedding."

"Wedding?" Jess's voice must have carried into the house, because everyone stopped talking. Then Randi noticed Jordan. She shrugged her shoulders, and Jordan smiled and went back to his conversation.

"Not yet, but maybe down the road."

"He must be some kind of a kisser for you to think marriage after just one."

"I've had several thoughts, but it isn't time yet."

"Right. You're bad—you know that? One kiss and you're sunk. But I have to agree he's a far better choice than Cal."

"Don't even go there."

"Unbelievable. I'm so glad you didn't marry him."

"You and me both. I feel sorry for him. I hope he finds the Lord and saves his relationship with his child."

Randi peeked into the living room. Only a few people remained. Jordan and Steve Healey were among them. He kept glancing out at her. "Jess, I want to talk with Jordan. Can you drive my car home tomorrow?"

"Sure."

Randi handed her keys to Jess. "Thanks."

They joined the others in the living room. "Can I get a lift home with you, Jordan?"

"Absolutely. But what about—?"

She held her finger to her lips, gave the international "sh" sign, then turned to Steve. "Did you come here on your motorcycle?"

"Yup."

"Can Jordan meet you at his place?"

"Well, I don't know. The sheriff said we weren't supposed to leave Jordan alone."

Randi slipped her arm around Jordan's elbow. "He won't be alone."

"Ah, well," Steve stammered.

Wayne Kearns cleared his throat. "Miranda, I believe you can use the telephone to talk with Jordan. And considering all that's been going on, it might be best that you two not spend too much time alone. If you catch my drift."

Perfectly. She wanted to scream.

Jordan placed his hand over Randi's. "Excuse us for a couple of minutes."

He led Randi out to the deck. "Honey, what's going on?"

"I'm sorry. I just want to spend time with you."

He wrapped her in his arms. "And I, you. But—" He kissed the top of her head.

Randi sighed. Her head was buzzing with conflicting emotions. "I'll call you after I get home."

"Good. Everything is going to be all right. Trust me."

Randi let out a nervous giggle. "I do."

❧

Jordan's emotions had run the full gamut today. He could only imagine Miranda's had done the same. Wayne Kearns in his not-so-diplomatic way was right; they shouldn't be alone tonight. Caution seemed to be the word for the hour.

Steve had followed him home from the Kearnses'. They talked briefly; then Steve sat down on the sofa and watched the Red Sox win. Jordan placed a call to Miranda and planned to meet her for breakfast in the morning.

Jordan took a hot shower and allowed the pulsing water to work out the remaining tension in his back. Even though the sheriff believed in him, the fact still remained that Agent Wilkes believed him guilty. And the very real possibility existed that he could be set up if the agent went rogue. *Please, Lord, prevent that from happening.*

He called his father and told him about his developing relationship with Miranda. "Dad, I want to marry her."

"Well, congratulations, son. Would you like your great-grandmother's engagement ring?"

"Really?"

"Sure. Let me check with your mother. Hang on." His father covered the phone with his hand. "Mom's all excited. She's picking up the extension."

"Jordan, is this the same girl you were talking about when you were here?"

"Yes."

His mother giggled. "I thought so. Your great-grandmother would love for your wife to wear her ring."

"I think Miranda would like it, too. It isn't your traditional engagement ring."

"No, it isn't," his father agreed. "But if her eyes are the same color as your great-grandmother's, I'd say it would be as beautiful on her as it was on your great-grandmother."

"Yeah, I believe so."

"So when do we get to meet our new daughter?" his mother asked.

"We're not married yet. I haven't asked her."

"All in good time, son," his father said. They talked for a few more minutes, and Jordan agreed to take a trip down to Boston with Miranda when things were settled in Maine concerning the missing child.

He hung up the phone, and it immediately rang. "Jordan, it's me."

"Miranda?"

"Yeah. Listen—I remembered something Mabel said to me. I'm going to check it out."

"Miranda, what are you going to do? Don't do anything foolish. Call Sheriff McKean. Tell him what you're thinking. What are you thinking?"

"Mabel said something about new neighbors. I'm going to check out the neighbors."

"Miranda, don't. Let the police handle it."

"I'll be careful. I'll just visit Mabel."

"Honey, it's late. How late does this woman stay up?"

"Half the night."

"Miranda, please—let the sheriff do this."

"I'll be careful."

"I don't like it. Please stay home."

"Jordan, you need to trust me."

Jordan groaned. This was the issue she had with him, and now she was turning the tables on him. "I still don't like it."

"I'll be fine. I grew up playing over there. I know all those roads."

"Be careful."

Jordan started to pace. He rubbed the back of his neck. He didn't like this. Not one bit. Duke watched him without moving. His eyes simply rolled back and forth, not missing one of Jordan's steps.

"I will. I love you."

"I love you, too. That's why I want you to be careful."

"I know, and I will. I'll call you in the morning."

"Call me when you return."

"It will be late."

"I don't care. Call me."

"Okay. Love you. Bye."

Jordan hung up the phone and fell on his knees. "Dear Lord, protect her."

❧

Randi ran down the dirt road and over to Mabel's house. No

lights were on. She wouldn't wake the older woman. She ran past the various houses that made up Mabel's neighborhood. A large dog barked. Randi kept running. Seeing nothing, she ran back to her car and called Jordan on her cell.

"Hey, it's me."

"Where are you?"

"At Mabel's. Everyone's asleep down here."

"Of course they are. It's midnight. Go home, Miranda. I'm not comfortable with you being out there."

"Okay." She turned on the car engine and popped the car into gear. "I'm heading home now."

In her rearview mirror, she saw a porch light come on at one of the houses. She continued to head back toward town.

"Miranda?"

"Huh? Oh, I'm fine. Sorry. A porch light went on. I was trying to catch someone in the rearview mirror."

"Honey, call Sheriff McKean."

"I will in the morning. 'Night, Jordan. Sorry for the disappointment."

Jordan let out a nervous chuckle. "I'm glad you're all right. These people abduct children for money. They can't be real nice, reasonable people."

She hadn't really thought about that. She'd only been thinking about Jordan and how to help him. "You're right. I'll call the sheriff."

"Good. I'll see you at breakfast."

"I'm looking forward to it." They hung up, and she called the sheriff's office. The answering machine came on. She left a detailed message about what Mabel had said about her new neighbors and hung up.

By the time she returned home, Agent Wilkes was standing at her door. "Are you insane?"

"Good evening to you, Agent Wilkes."

"Look, lady. I don't care what you think of Jordan Lamont or me, but you can't go running off in the middle of the night looking for trouble. Didn't your parents teach you anything?"

"Nothing happened. I'm fine."

"This time. But what's to prevent you from doing something as foolish again in the future?"

"I don't need a lecture from a man who doesn't obey the rules either."

"Excuse me?"

Randi paled.

"Do you have a videotape of Jordan and me kissing?"

"What? Who's feeding you this stuff?"

"I was hoping you might. Be nice for our memory book in the future. Look—I'm fine."

"I can see that. Miss Blake, I need your word you'll stay out of this investigation. We can't have you tipping off the suspects."

"Are you saying you believe Jordan?"

"I won't go that far, but he obviously doesn't have the child."

He relaxed his stance. "By the way, for the record, I do have a judge's order now to listen in on Jordan's phone conversations. And if something had happened to you tonight, you'd have been glad I did. Fortunately the sheriff knew who you were talking about and headed out there."

"I didn't see him."

Agent Wilkes laughed. "You jogged through the neighborhood."

Randi's legs felt like rubber.

"Stay out of there, Miss Blake. For the sake of the child, stay away."

"Yes, sir."

Randi walked past Agent Wilkes into the house. She wondered who else had seen her out there. She hadn't noticed anyone. She showered and went to bed. What had she been thinking?

nineteen

Tired from a restless night, Jordan went to the kitchen to prepare breakfast. The idea of Miranda trying to find the child last night in the dark on her own caused an ulcer to develop in one night. Well, maybe not a full-blown ulcer, but close.

He had a frying pan in one hand and a mixing bowl in the other when Steve Healey walked in. " 'Morning."

"Did you sleep well?"

"Not exactly. Couches and I never seem to get along all that well. How about yourself?"

Steve was probably a few years younger than his dad. *I should have offered to sleep on the couch.* "Sorry you were so uncomfortable. As for me, nada. Miranda decided to go out to see someone named Mabel in search of her new neighbors." Jordan set the frying pan down on the stove, placed the mixing bowl on the counter, and pulled out some eggs, milk, cheese, onions, peppers, ham, and potatoes.

"Miranda?"

"Sorry. Randi." He set the refrigerator items on the counter next to the mixing bowl and fetched his cutting board and knife.

"Oh, right. As for Mabel, that would be Mabel Bishop. She's eighty-something and doesn't look a day over sixty-five. She works at the post office." Jordan set a mug of black coffee in front of Steve. "She has more energy than most people half her age, me included."

Jordan searched for the grater in the lower cabinet where he kept it. "I'd like to meet her one day."

"You probably will. Whatcha cooking?" Steve picked up

the coffee and sipped it, not bothering to add cream or sugar.

"I thought I'd make some hash-browned potatoes and an omelet. Mir—Randi is coming for breakfast. If you have the time, I'd love to make you something. A thank-you for being my babysitter last night."

Steve laughed. "I was out pretty quickly. But I'm glad I could help. I appreciate the offer for breakfast, but I should get going." He hesitated.

"Are you sure? Can I fix something for you to take with you? At least let me give you some coffee to go," Jordan said. Having found the grater, he placed it on the counter on top of the cutting board.

"Nothing, really." Steve hesitated. "I'm not sure if I'm supposed to wait here until someone else comes."

"Oh." The idea of having to have someone with him around the clock hadn't appealed last night, and this morning it annoyed him. "I'm fine. Miranda will be here shortly. What could go wrong?"

"You're sure?"

"Absolutely. Go on."

"Okay, catch ya later." Steve finished his coffee, put on his faded Boston Red Sox cap, and headed out the door.

Jordan went back to work organizing his breakfast with Miranda. All the prep work was done when the phone rang.

"Hello."

"Jordan, this is Sheriff McKean. We caught them early this morning."

"Praise the Lord! Is the little girl safe and unharmed?"

"She's safe."

Jordan knew Lucy Tomisson had been kidnapped for ransom, and usually the victims were kept in good health, unlike other abductions. "I'm really glad to hear this. Does that mean I'm clear of any charges from Agent Wilkes?"

The sheriff chuckled. "More than likely he's trying to pull his foot out of his mouth right now. I hope this is the end of it for you. And, more important, it's the end of it for this child. Her parents should be arriving up here in about four more hours."

"I'd love to photograph that reunion."

"I'll keep that in mind."

"Sorry, Sheriff. I was speaking out loud. I'm not asking to be an intrusion on their family time. I just know there will be some mighty happy faces on both parents and child."

"More than likely. All right. I've got a lot of paperwork to complete, but I thought you'd like to know."

"Thanks. I appreciate it."

Jordan hung up the phone. "At least I don't have to have a babysitter any longer," he thought aloud. Jordan made several calls, letting his parents, Dena, and others know the child had been found. He waited to tell Miranda in person.

Just then she knocked on the screen door, still wearing her running clothes. "Jordan, did you hear?"

So much for the surprise. "Yes, the sheriff called."

"Isn't it wonderful!" She stepped through the back door and into the kitchen.

"Yes, it's an answer to our prayers. Come here." He opened his arms.

"No, no, I can't. I'm all sweaty. I just wanted you to know."

"Thanks. So should I hold off on breakfast?"

"Oh, no, I forgot. I'm sorry. I ran seven miles this morning. Agent Wilkes scared the living daylights out of me last night."

Jordan's spine went rigid. "Why? What did he do? What happened?"

"Oh, nothing. He informed me that the sheriff and others saw me jogging through Mabel's neighborhood last night." Miranda walked over to the window. "I didn't even see them. What if the criminals had been watching and had seen me? I could have—"

Jordan closed the distance between them, wrapping her in

his arms. "Shh. It's all right. You're okay. Nothing happened."
Not that it couldn't have. Fear washed over him at the thought
of losing her. His heart pounded. His mind filled with an
urgent desire to ask her to marry him, right now, right here.
Then the sensible part of his mind kicked in and told him
now was not the time. Soon, but the right time and place
needed to be prayed about and certainly planned. Didn't all
women want a special proposal?

Miranda snuggled into Jordan's embrace and released a
pent-up breath. She leaned against him for a moment then
jumped back. "I'm so sorry. I forgot. I soiled your clothes."

Jordan reached out and pulled her back. "They'll wash.
Kiss me."

Miranda giggled and complied.

❧

Randi ran home and got ready for work. Jordan made her
breakfast to go and wrapped her omelet in a soft tortilla
so she could eat and drive at the same time. She wanted to
cancel going to the restaurant, but she still needed the money
to pay her rent. Her savings were beginning to add up; with
any luck, she could start considering purchasing a home
instead of renting. She was thankful for Jordan's suggestions
on how to handle her finances. All she needed was a small
cottage for herself. Then it hit her. What about a home with
Jordan? Children? Oh, yeah, a small cottage would not be
enough.

The rest of the day, she entertained thoughts about marrying Jordan, imagining arguing over how they should wait and
get to know one another better.

She wanted to get together with Jordan that evening, but
she had to work on the Web pages for her clients. At home,
she sat down with a sandwich, a glass of iced tea, and her
computer. An hour later, she heard a knock at her door.

"Hey."

Jordan stood there, as handsome as ever.

"Man, I love your eyes."

Randi giggled. He'd been obsessed with her eyes since the first day they met. "Come in. I'm working, but I can visit for a while."

"I was hoping you'd say that."

"So what's happening with the missing girl? Have you heard anything?"

"The parents came to town this afternoon. They're staying at Montgomery's Bed-and-Breakfast for the night. No one has released to the media that she's been found. They're going to do that tomorrow so the family can have a day without media interruption."

"And, of course, the FBI will want to question the child."

"Of course," Jordan grumbled.

"He was only doing his job," Randi reminded him gently.

"I know. But I hope he treats the little girl much better than he did me."

She walked over to him and kissed his cheek. "He will. They've been trained in how to help the victims."

The doorbell rang. Randi excused herself and went to answer it. Agent Wilkes stood there with his shoulders squared. "May I speak with Jordan Lamont, please?"

"How'd—?" She stopped. They wouldn't still be listening in on them, would they? "Jordan!" she called back to the kitchen.

Jordan came to the door. "Agent Wilkes? What can I do for you?"

"May I come in?"

Jordan looked at Randi. She nodded. What else did one say to the FBI?

"Mr. Lamont." Agent Wilkes looked like a hermit crab that was afraid to come out of its shell. "I want to express my apologies for anything I said or did during the course of my investigation that caused you anxiety. I was wrong. I made assumptions and didn't examine all the facts. I'm sorry. And

I know it's a little too late, but I want to thank you for taking those pictures. Without them, we wouldn't have little Lucy."

"You're welcome. And you're forgiven."

"Thank you." Agent Wilkes cleared his throat. "Sheriff McKean has asked for you to come down to Montgomery's Bed-and-Breakfast. The family would like to meet you. Oh, and they asked for you to bring your camera."

"Al–l–l–l ri–i–ight," Jordan said, drawing out the words. "Can Miranda come also?"

"Yes, both of you are part of why we found the little girl."

"We'll be there shortly."

"Very good. And seriously, I am sorry for giving you such a hard time. I don't know what came over me. I promise it won't happen again. We could have lost her if—"

Jordan placed his hand on Wilkes's shoulder. "It's all right. She's alive, and the Lord allowed us to find her. That's all that matters."

Agent Wilkes gave a halfhearted smile and nodded before walking out the door.

"Do you have your cameras?" Randi asked.

Jordan laughed. "You don't know me all that well yet, honey, but the first thing you need to know is that I always have at least one camera with me, and generally two or three."

Randi came up beside him. "Well, we'd better go, because I have a lot of work to do today."

He wrapped his arms around her and yawned. "Nighttime can't come soon enough. I didn't sleep much last night."

"You're not the only one."

"No, I imagine the sheriff and his crew are wasted, too. And tomorrow the media will descend on Squabbin Bay, and the locals won't know what to do with 'em."

❧

They met with the grateful parents for a brief visit and had a chance to get acquainted with Lucy. Jordan took some publicity photos and planned to make copies available to the media in the morning. At midnight, they released the news that Lucy Tomisson was safe and sound, along with details of her rescue.

The family had listened to the advice given by other families in similar circumstances. Jordan's pictures would be the only ones released to the media. Randi hoped the media would respect the family's wishes. Considering it wasn't a high-profile case, a horde of journalists and photographers wasn't trying from every angle to take a picture of the family. By the time the father gave the press conference, Lucy and her mother were safe and sound in another town out of reach.

The next few weeks kept Randi and Jordan squeaking out moments of time for one another. With fall approaching, she made plans to show him Acadia National Park. They packed a cooler and headed south. One day after they married, she hoped to go camping with Jordan at the park.

With his Jeep packed, they drove down the highway. "So tell me what it is about Acadia that you love? I've seen pictures, and it looks awesome, but why does it interest you?"

"I love camping, and it's just like, well, the perfect example of Maine's rustic coast. I don't know why it's such a special place to me. My family and I have gone there so many times over the years. We love it."

"Hmm, I'm looking forward to it. Of course, it could be you love it because of the memories."

"No doubt."

"Oh, by the way, my parents are looking forward to our visit next week."

"I can't wait. I'm terrified, but I can't wait." Randi squirmed in her seat.

"Terrified? Why?"

"Because they're your parents."

"They already like you."

She smiled. "So you say."

"Hey, now, have I ever steered you wrong?"

ﹽ

The ring weighed heavily in Jordan's pocket. He hoped and prayed today would be the day for another favorite memory for Miranda in Acadia National Park. Today was the first full day they'd managed to have with one another since Lucy Tomisson was found.

"No." Miranda pulled her legs to her chest and held them. It amused him that she was so nervous at the prospect of meeting his parents.

"Miranda, I love you."

Her smile brightened. "I love you, too. I can't believe how busy we've been the past few weeks."

"Neither can I. I'm truly sorry Lucy was kidnapped from her home, but it has helped launch my photo journalism career. Dena says she's booked me on several shoots, and many more are pending."

"How long will you be gone?" Her voice sounded sad.

"Each shoot is different. Is it a problem?"

"Jordan, I don't want to come across like a wet sponge, but how often will you travel? I mean. . ."

"How often will I be home with you?"

"Yeah, if we get married."

Jordan smiled. *If* was no longer a question in his mind, but rather *when*. "I'll take only as many trips as we agree upon. Before we marry, I'd like to accept as many assignments as possible. My first obligation is to Dena and the studio, so I can't take more than two or so a month."

"I'm only starting to get a handle on how a photographer makes money, but are these trips that worthwhile?"

Jordan chuckled. "Most of the time, yes. Some trips, like the one to the Sudan, won't produce a lot of income."

"Jordan, what's changed? When we were first getting to know one another, you told me about your plan to earn so much and have a house *before* you marry. Are you expecting us to wait years?"

He tightened his grip on the steering wheel. "No, I'm not wanting to wait years. But I do think a little planning and some savings would be helpful, don't you?"

"Yes. In fact, you'll be happy to know I started a savings account after you challenged me, and I'm happy to say I have a nice little amount set aside."

"Wonderful. Money issues have been a problem for me for as long as I can remember. I appreciate my parents' influence, but they drummed it into my head for so long it's almost second nature to me. I'll always be a planner, but I'm trying to be more flexible."

"Oops. Sorry. Turn right up here."

Jordan turned into the entrance to the park. Without question, the area was stunning.

"There's no way for you to see the entire park in one day, so I thought we'd hike up Cadillac Mountain."

"You're bound and determined to have me exercise, aren't you?"

She wiggled her eyebrows. His stomach flipped. "Probably." She winked.

They drove up Park Loop Road and parked. "What about Duke?"

"He'll be fine. Trust me," she said as she bounced out of the vehicle.

"Come on, boy. We're in for it today." Jordan attached a leash and knew he'd be carrying Duke most of the way. His stubby little legs could not keep up with Miranda's sleek ones.

"You tricked me," Jordan protested. The road went right to the top of the mountain.

"Possibly."

"Wow! It's an awesome view."

"Yeah, it's pretty amazing." Miranda beamed. "There's such variety here. The ocean, the mountains, the sandy beach, the rocky beach, little streams—it's all here in one spot. There's a place over there"—she pointed to her left—"where the waves splash against the rocks and the water spews out like a geyser."

"I would love to see it." *Man, I hope she doesn't want a long engagement.*

She placed her hand in his. "I want to show you. I want..." She paused then continued. "Jordan, I know we don't see eye-to-eye on financial matters. Is this going to be a problem for us?"

He wrapped her in his arms. "I wondered that myself a while back. I don't believe it will be, if we are honest and open with one another about our feelings and agree on how to handle our differences ahead of time. I told you about my parents encouraging me with regard to my income before marriage."

She nodded.

"Well, it turns out I misunderstood what they were telling me. They set an example, and I took it as gospel."

"So are you saying you can consider marriage before you buy your own home?"

Jordan let out a nervous chuckle. Duke barked. "Yes and no. I'm wondering if we could start looking for a place together."

"I'd love to help you look."

"No. I mean—Miranda, I'm getting this all wrong. Hang on a minute." He released her and bent down on one knee.

Miranda's eyes widened. The deep pools in her eyes glistened. "What I'm trying to say is, I'm not perfect. I have many flaws. I don't have a huge income. But would you do me the honor of becoming my wife?"

Miranda blinked twice.

Jordan reached into his pocket and touched the small gold band that had belonged to his great-grandmother.

"Miranda?"

She started to shake. "Are you sure?"

"Absolutely. I've known since the second day I met you that

I wanted you to be my wife."

Miranda swallowed hard.

Jordan's fingers started to sweat holding the ring.

"How long of an engagement?"

Jordan let out a nervous chuckle. "I wasn't planning on a long wait. But it's up to you. You can set the date."

"Tomorrow?"

"If you wish. I'd marry you right here and now."

"Jordan, are you sure? Absolutely, positively sure?"

"Yes. I love you, Miranda Blake, with all my heart and soul. You make me complete. Please say you'll marry me."

"Yes! Yes! Of course I will."

Jordan jumped up and took her in his arms. His lips captured hers, and the kiss deepened. Duke pawed at them then barked. "Sorry, boy. But what do you think of Miranda being your mom?"

Duke barked again.

Miranda giggled. "You'd better tell him he's not coming to the wedding or on the honeymoon."

Jordan held her close. "Of course he won't. He'll be house-sitting. So, seriously, when do you want to get married?"

"Tomorrow. But I think our parents would have a fit."

"Agreed." Jordan fingered the ring once again. "Miranda, I have a ring. It belonged to my great-grandmother. As you saw in the photograph, her eyes were as dark as yours. My great-grandfather bought her this ring to go with her eyes. I'm hoping you'll like it and accept it as your engagement ring. If you want the traditional diamond I'll understand, but. . ." He pulled out the ring and slipped it on her finger.

"Oh, Jordan, it's beautiful."

A black pearl encircled by tiny diamonds made up the unique ring. "You like it?"

"Yes. It's beautiful. This was your great-grandmother's?"

"Yes. Great-grandfather told the story of searching the world for his perfect mate and the perfect ring for her. Now, we all know he was not a world traveler, but he loved to make up exotic tales of searching for the love of his life. When he found her, he gave her the black pearl because it was rare, and he cherished my great-grandmother as a rare jewel. Miranda, you're that same rare jewel I've searched my whole life for. Please accept this ring as a token of my love for you and how special you are to me."

Her eyes filled with tears. Unable to speak, she simply nodded her head. Jordan kissed her delicate pink lips again and thanked the Lord for such a special woman in his life.

epilogue

Nine months later

Randi stood in Pastor Russell's office waiting for Jess. Jordan's brother, Adam, had called her out of the room moments before. Randi never could have believed she'd be this nervous waiting for the organ to play.

Jess opened the door.

"Is everything all right?" Randi asked.

"Yeah. Um, how big of a deal is it for Duke not to be at your wedding?"

"You're kidding, right?"

Jess shook her head.

Uncontrollable laughter spilled out. "Of course he'd bring Duke. How did Jordan get Duke past Pastor Russell?"

"Uh, he didn't."

"Huh?"

"Well, it's my fault really."

"Jess?"

Jess shrugged. "He just seemed like part of the family, and since Pastor Russell is my mom's son and my stepbrother, what can he do to me?"

"What have you done, Jess?" Jess was her maid of honor. Randi just smiled and wondered if maybe she should have made a different choice.

"Trust me—he'll be good."

Randi shook her head. "You're one of a kind, Jess."

"So are you, Randi. I'm so happy for the two of you."

"Thanks."

The organ music started to play. Randi's mother stood in

the doorway. "Everything all right, dear?"

"Yes, Mom, thanks." Her mother blew her a kiss and left.

Jordan's parents were wonderful, too. She had loved them from the moment she met them.

Jess looped her arm around Randi's.

Her father slipped through the door. "Miranda, you're beautiful. You take my breath away."

"Thanks, Dad."

Jess squeezed her arm and kissed her on the cheek then left the room to line up for the processional.

"How you doing, kiddo?" her dad asked.

"Fine."

"That nervous, huh?"

"Does it show?"

"A little. But, hey, it happens to all of us. Once you're standing next to Jordan and you take his hand, it will all wash away. At least it did for your mother and me."

Randi kissed his cheek. "Thanks, Dad. I love you."

"I love you, too, sweetheart. But it's time."

He led her through the door and down the hall. The organ music shifted to the traditional bridal march. Everyone stood. Randi looked down the aisle. Jordan stood there as handsome as ever, his hair tied back. Duke sat beside Jordan, wearing his own bowtie and tuxedo tails. She smiled. Jess was right. Duke belonged here.

Jordan's smile broadened. Her gaze stayed fixed on his. Today they would unite as one. Today they would break down all the barriers of their hearts, no longer trespassers but welcomed and honored guests

At the altar, she whispered, "I love you."

"I love you, too." He held out his hand. And it was as her father had said—all fears washed away.

Today was the beginning of their future, and Randi couldn't have been happier.

A Letter To Our Readers

Dear Reader:

In order that we might better contribute to your reading enjoyment, we would appreciate your taking a few minutes to respond to the following questions. We welcome your comments and read each form and letter we receive. When completed, please return to the following:

Fiction Editor
Heartsong Presents
PO Box 719
Uhrichsville, Ohio 44683

1. Did you enjoy reading *Trespassed Hearts* by Lynn A. Coleman?
   ❑ Very much! I would like to see more books by this author!
   ❑ Moderately. I would have enjoyed it more if

   _____

   _____

   _____

2. Are you a member of **Heartsong Presents**? ❑ Yes ❑ No
   If no, where did you purchase this book? _____

   _____

3. How would you rate, on a scale from 1 (poor) to 5 (superior), the cover design? _____

4. On a scale from 1 (poor) to 10 (superior), please rate the following elements.

   _____ Heroine   _____ Plot
   _____ Hero   _____ Inspirational theme
   _____ Setting   _____ Secondary characters

5. These characters were special because? _____

_____

_____

6. How has this book inspired your life? _____

_____

_____

7. What settings would you like to see covered in future
   Heartsong Presents books? _____

_____

_____

8. What are some inspirational themes you would like to see
   treated in future books? _____

_____

_____

9. Would you be interested in reading other **Heartsong
   Presents** titles? ❏ Yes ❏ No

10. Please check your age range:

    ❏ Under 18   ❏ 18-24

    ❏ 25-34   ❏ 35-45

    ❏ 46-55   ❏ Over 55

Name _____

Occupation _____

Address _____

City, State, Zip _____

Heart♥ng

Presents

Great Inspirational Romance at a Great Price!

Heartsong Presents books are inspirational romances in contemporary and historical settings, designed to give you an enjoyable, spirit-lifting reading experience. You can choose wonderfully written titles from some of today's best authors like Wanda E. Brunstetter, Mary Connealy, Susan Page Davis, Cathy Marie Hake, Joyce Livingston, and many others.

When ordering quantities less than twelve, above titles are $2.97 each.
Not all titles may be available at time of order.

SEND TO: **Heartsong Presents** Readers' Service
P.O. Box 721, Uhrichsville, Ohio 44683

Please send me the items checked above. I am enclosing $ _____
(please add $3.00 to cover postage per order. OH add 7% tax. NJ
add 6%). Send check or money order, no cash or C.O.D.s, please.
To place a credit card order, call 1-740-922-7280.

NAME _____

ADDRESS _____

CITY/STATE _____ ZIP _____

HP 2-08

HEARTSONG
PRESENTS

If you love Christian romance...

$10.⁹⁹

You'll love Heartsong Presents' inspiring and faith-filled romances by today's very best Christian authors. . .Wanda E. Brunstetter, Mary Connealy, Susan Page Davis, Cathy Marie Hake, and Joyce Livingston, to mention a few!

When you join Heartsong Presents, you'll enjoy four brand-new, mass market, 176-page books—two contemporary and two historical—that will build you up in your faith when you discover God's role in every relationship you read about!

Mass Market 176 Pages

Imagine. . .four new romances every four weeks—with men and women like you who long to meet the one God has chosen as the love of their lives…all for the low price of $10.99 postpaid.

To join, simply visit www.heartsong presents.com or complete the coupon below and mail it to the address provided.

✂- -

YES! Sign me up for Heart♥ng!

NEW MEMBERSHIPS WILL BE SHIPPED IMMEDIATELY!
Send no money now. We'll bill you only $10.99 postpaid with your first shipment of four books. Or for faster action, call 1-740-922-7280.

NAME _____

ADDRESS_____

CITY_____ STATE _____ ZIP _____

MAIL TO: HEARTSONG PRESENTS, P.O. Box 721, Uhrichsville, Ohio 44683
or sign up at WWW.HEARTSONGPRESENTS.COM